PENGUIN BOOKS

Lost City of the Templars

With the tents up and darkness falling quickly over the jungle, Holliday noticed that Tanaki was crouched by the water's edge, dragging his fingers through the water. Holliday joined him, squatting down beside the Indian. From his expression, there was no doubt something was bothering him.

'What's the matter?' Holliday asked.

Tanaki lifted his fingers out of the water and rubbed them together. 'Oil,' he said.

'Could it be from the Zodiacs?'

'Look,' said Tanaki. In the last of the fading light, Holliday could see a shimmering iridescent slick that began well ahead of their landing spot. 'It comes from above the high water,' said Tanaki.

'An outboard from some little village upstream?'

'The only villages upstream belong to the Kayapo, who have no boats with engines, and anyway, the oil is much too heavy.'

'An airplane?' asked Holliday.

'I think so, and not too far from here or the oil would have been carried to the middle of the stream and would not be so visible.'

'We've got trouble, then.'

'Bad trouble.' Tanaki nodded. 'Very bad.'

Also by Paul Christopher:

Michelangelo's Notebook
The Lucifer Gospel
Rembrandt's Ghost
The Aztec Heresy
The Sword of the Templars
The Templar Cross
The Templar Throne
The Templar Conspiracy
The Templar Legion
Red Templar
Valley of the Templars

Lost City of the Templars

PAUL CHRISTOPHER

PENGUIN BOOKS

PENGUIN BOOKS

Published by the Penguin Group
Penguin Books Ltd, 80 Strand, London WC2R ORL, England
Penguin Group (USA) Inc., 375 Hudson Street, New York, New York 10014, USA
Penguin Group (Canada), 90 Eglinton Avenue East, Suite 700, Toronto, Ontario,
Canada M4P 2Y3 (a division of Pearson Penguin Canada Inc.)
Penguin Ireland, 25 St Stephen's Green, Dublin 2, Ireland
(a division of Penguin Books Ltd)
Penguin Group (Australia), 707 Collins Street, Melbourne, Victoria 3008, Australia
(a division of Pearson Australia Group Pty Ltd)
Penguin Books India Pvt Ltd, 11 Community Centre, Panchsheel Park,
New Delhi – 110 017, India
Penguin Group (NZ), 67 Apollo Drive, Rosedale, Auckland 0632, New Zealand
(a division of Pearson New Zealand Ltd)
Penguin Books (South Africa) (Pty) Ltd, Block D, Rosebank Office Park,
181 Jan Smuts Avenue, Parktown North, Gauteng 2193, South Africa

Penguin Books Ltd, Registered Offices: 80 Strand, London WC2R ORL, England

www.penguin.com

First published in the USA by Signet, an imprint of New American Library,
a division of Penguin Group (USA) Inc. 2013
First published in Great Britain in Penguin Books 2014

001

Set in 13/15.25pt Garamond MT Std
Typeset by Jouve (UK), Milton Keynes
Printed in England by Clays Ltd, St Ives plc

ISBN: 978-0-718-17729-4

www.greenpenguin.co.uk

Penguin Books is committed to a sustainable
future for our business, our readers and our planet.
This book is made from Forest Stewardship
Council™ certified paper.

This one is for my grandson, Gabriel,
in hopes that he will enjoy
Sherlock Holmes and Professor Challenger
as much as I did.

When you have eliminated the impossible, whatever remains, however improbable, must be the truth.

Sherlock Holmes

Things are only impossible until they're not.

Jean-Luc Picard, *Star Trek:*
The Next Generation

Into what dangers would you lead me, Cassius,
That you would have me seek into myself
For that which is not in me?

William Shakespeare, *Julius Caesar*,
Act I, Scene I

Prologue

Montevideo, Uruguay
Mouth of the Rio de la Plata
August 26, 1928

Even now, after almost three years in the jungle, the young man retained his chiseled, almost movie star good looks – Douglas Fairbanks on a very bad night perhaps, or on a very good morning after. Tall, dark and handsome, his freshly shaven cheeks showing the paler skin where there had lately been a beard. But there were lines on his face that had not been there three years ago when the expedition began, and there was a hardness and a cruelty in the set of his square jaw and the bitter light in his jade-colored eyes.

He'd arrived in Montevideo penniless and exhausted. The penniless part had been dealt with easily enough by selling a dozen of the gold coins to a bullion dealer on the Punta del Este. The old dealer asked no questions about why a young bearded man with the stink of the jungle on him and the yellowish cast of malaria in his face would be selling thirteenth-century coins from Genoa, Italy. The dealer simply handed over a thick wad of pale purple five-hundred-peso banknotes to the young man and bade him a fast farewell before he changed his mind.

The exhausted part would be taken care of on the three-week-long passage home. The young man had slept in a seaman's hotel in the warehouse district close to the docks the night before and had arrived at the terminal just after dawn. The huge bulk of the Royal Mail Steam Packet ship *Almanzora* loomed over him in the morning mist off the steaming river like a dream, her single orange funnel and her long black hull the cradle that would take him home.

When the purser blew his whistle, he was the first man up the gangway, the newly purchased leather case with the even newer suits of clothing light as a feather in his hand, the heavy metal footlocker with its hidden treasures even lighter on his shoulders.

He had paid for a first-class cabin on the promenade deck, well forward of the funnel to keep the soot off his clothes. The cabin was more than ample for his needs. The walls were paneled in patterned fruitwood, the deck was covered with patterned wall-to-wall carpeting and there was a wide bed with sideboards to prevent accidents if the ship rolled or pitched too much in the night. There was a dressing table, a built-in cupboard, a couch, several chairs for guests and most important of all an adjoining private, tiled bathroom with a large ceramic tub, a sink and a large mirror.

The young man set the suitcase on the floor and heaved the footlocker up on to the bed. Fishing out the leather thong that hung around his neck and slipping it over his head, the young man used the single key on the thong to open the box. He threw back the lid and examined the contents, removing them, one by one. First came the string-bound bundle of twenty-three of the russet-colored *Pierce's Memorandum and Accounts* notebooks that the colonel favored. To one side was the foot-long bamboo tube that still contained at least a hundred of the remaining one-ounce gold pieces, stopped from rattling by the plug of a bloodstained rag. Jack's blood.

He lifted out the bamboo tube and the bundle of notebooks, putting them to one side. Beneath them was a large leather bag made from a capybara, the hog-sized rodent that lived its life foraging in the rainforests of Brazil. The bag was easily the size of a bulging fist. The young man lifted the bag out of the footlocker and set it on his knees. He loosened the leather ties that kept the bag shut and reached in an open hand.

He pulled out a fistful of emeralds, sapphires and a single-faceted diamond as big as a robin's egg. A fortune in his hand, and hundreds more like them still in the bag. Enough to last a man several lifetimes, every day of those lifetimes haunted by the toll the gemstones had taken on his soul. He dropped the stones back into the sack, tightened the thong and tied it off, then set the bag aside on the bed with the other items.

At the very bottom of the footlocker was the greatest treasure of all: a box, hand-carved from the wood of a jacaranda and set with a silver clasp. The box was a little more than a foot and a half wide and two feet long, just barely fitting into the bottom of the footlocker. He lifted the box out of the footlocker and laid it gently across his knees. In the corridor outside his cabin door, he heard a steward calling out the 'All ashore that's going ashore' in English, Portuguese and Spanish.

A few moments later the ship gave a single blast of its whistle and the young man faintly heard the sound of the gangway rattling back into the *Almanzora*'s great black hull. The vibration of the engines far below his feet turned to a deeper note, and he was vaguely aware that they were moving. He was on his way home now and finally he was safe.

He undid the clasp and pushed back the lid of the box. The sight of its contents was still enough to make him draw in his breath. Inside, carefully dried in sawdust for several weeks, was the head, thorax and abdomen of what had lately been a living creature pinned to the felt bottom of the box. Neatly set alongside it were the twenty-two-inch silvery wings that had once set the magnificent insect to flight.

It was, without a doubt, a perfect specimen of a *Meganeuropsis permiana*, a giant, flesh-eating dragonfly that had been extinct for the last two hundred and fifty million years.

I

If you were looking for a word to describe Peggy Blackstock's mood as she walked down the Strand in the seaside English town of Torquay, 'bored' would spring to your lips, immediately followed by, 'If I see one more Ye Olde English Pub advertising the best fish and chips in Torquay, I'm going to hurl.'

She'd been in town for two days, and there were still three more to go until Rafi's World Archaeology Congress convention was over. She was already at her wits' end. Being in Torquay was like being in Coney Island without Nathan's, the Cyclone or the bumper cars. There were just as many people, but the sand on the few beaches was muddy and dirty, the English Channel water was freezing cold and most of the food tasted like library paste.

It wasn't that she wasn't interested in her husband's work; in fact, she was more than interested – she was fascinated. Rafi specialized in the archaeology of the Crusades in Israel, and it took them both to dozens of sites from Jerusalem and Jaffa to Turkey and Turin, from Bosnia to Berlin and just about everywhere else in Europe. The Crusades had covered a lot of ground from the tenth century to the fourteenth and had reached as far as Sweden in their scope.

On her far-flung trips with Rafi, Peggy had become an accomplished archaeological photographer, and she landed more than enough freelance assignments, contributing pictures to *The New York Times Travel Magazine*, *Bon Appétit*, *National Geographic* and half a dozen other periodicals.

But something was missing, and Peggy knew exactly what it was: she craved the adrenaline rush of the truly unknown. Since coming back from Africa and losing track of her cousin Doc, she'd missed the . . . excitement and adventure that seemed to follow the ex-U.S. Army Ranger. It had been like that even when she was a girl.

It was Doc who'd taught her not to be afraid of heights and had calmly and efficiently taught her the skills of rock climbing in the Adirondacks. It was Doc who'd also taught her to hunt and fish and use a gun.

It was their uncle Henry the professor who'd given Peggy her first camera and taught her how to use it, but it was Doc who'd given her the courage to reach the places where she'd taken the first photographs that really mattered to her – the summit of Mt Skylight, fourth highest mountain in the Adirondacks, at sunset, a lone gray wolf in the winter at Yellowstone and a hibernating twelve-hundred-pound Kodiak bear in Alaska. It was Doc who'd started her on a lifelong quest for adventure, and somehow she knew the quest wasn't over yet.

One thing was sure: no one was going to find the adventure of a lifetime on the main street of Torquay, so at the next corner she turned left, away from the sea, and began climbing a narrow residential street of low attached bungalow-style dwellings that climbed up a seriously steep hill. It was not the most likely path to any kind of adventure at all, but the kids in the Narnia books found it through a cupboard door and Harry Potter found it on Platform 9 at King's Cross Station, so you never really knew, then, did you? Anyway, the exercise would do her good; she'd had one too many orders of Ye Olde fish and chips in the last few days.

There were a few shops on her way up the street; the English version of a 7-Eleven, with ads for fruity-flavored vodka coolers in the window. There was a hairstylist called British Hairways where the customers under their dryers looked as though they were all in their eighties, and a prosthetics store called Lend You a Hand with a single bright pink artificial leg in an otherwise empty window. She'd probably find the Bates Motel around the next bend.

What she did find was Weatherby and Sons Auction House, a ragtag assembly of a plastered bungalow attached to something at the rear that might have been a two-storey carriage house turned into a commercial garage and a third stumpy-looking building with a pair of firmly closed barn-sized doors.

Between the stumpy building and the garage lay a paved driveway that seemed to be doubling as a parking lot. At the end of the drive was an overhead aluminum door, slid three-quarters open. The roll-up door had a sign over it that read AUCTION TODAY. The car in the parking lot was a Jaguar XKR convertible – this year's model. The auction business was doing well by somebody. Peggy turned down the drive and ducked under the aluminum door.

The interior of the auction house was like the biggest, most chaotic yard sale in the world. Rowboats sat in the rafters, chandeliers and harpoons hanging from the beams, a stack of twisted narwhal tusks in one corner along with an equal number of ancient-looking bamboo fly rods and an enormous stuffed Scottish stag with a rack of eighteen-point antlers. The stag looked dusty, the glass eyes cloudy. Probably not a lot of buyers for stuffed giant Scottish stags in these days of fiscal responsibility. There was a stage at the front of the hall and perhaps a hundred or so folding chairs in front of it, most of them filled with people waving numbered paddles around as they bid on one item after another. Easels were set up on the stage to display works of art. There was a movable display wall full of hanging musical instruments and several tables with smaller and medium-sized objects to be sold. The auctioneer stood at a podium in the center of the stage and a crew of workers, male and female, carted things on and off the raised platform. An old man with grizzled stubble and thin hair slicked back with something that looked like Vaseline handed her a paddle and said, 'There you go, dearie. Have fun,' and pointed her to an empty seat at the end of an aisle halfway to the auction stage. She took her seat and noticed that the number on her paddle was 666, not a particularly auspicious number for someone who'd shivered her way through all five of the *Omen* movies.

The items went by quickly – six Regency chairs for twenty-two hundred pounds, the lot, a Georgian silver porringer for a thousand, a Royal Winton Circus jug for three hundred and sixty pounds . . . The list went on and on. Throughout every lot that went up, Peggy noticed that the paddle in the lap of the man beside her never twitched. He was in his fifties, with the high cheekbones and deep-set, dark eyes of a Russian or a Slav. His hair was too long – well over the nape of his neck, but his salt-and-pepper beard was perfectly groomed and the suit looked very expensive. The man's hands were strong, well manicured, but with the raw knuckles and the calluses of someone who spent a lot of time outdoors. He certainly didn't give the impression of someone who'd be interested in silver porridge pots. After fifteen minutes he made a frustrated grunting sound, stood up and left.

The next lot was a hodgepodge of household effects from a man named Raleigh Miller, who, according to the auctioneer, had lived to the ripe old age of a hundred and ten in a room at the back of the Hole in the Wall Pub on Park Lane for as long as anyone could remember. He came down to the pub each evening for a bottle of Samuel Smith's Imperial Stout and an order of fish and chips, both of which he took back to his room.

The room must have been sparsely furnished because there weren't too many household goods being offered and even fewer being auctioned. The final lot was a small steel footlocker, padlocked and rusted shut with a faded first-class travel sticker that said R.M.S.P. *ALMANZORA*. The apparent journey the box had taken was from Montevideo, Uruguay, to Southampton, arriving on 26 August, 1928. Peggy did the math. If Miller had been a hundred and ten years old when he died, that meant he'd been born in 1903. He'd been just twenty-five years old when he departed on the R.M.S.P. *Almanzora*. What was a twenty-five-year-old British kid doing in Uruguay, and where did he get the money for a first-class cabin? Interesting questions. The first price from the podium was two pounds. Peggy held up her paddle.

No one else bid. Once, twice, thrice and it was hers. She went down to the stage, paid her two pounds, filled out the appropriate paperwork and was given her prize. It weighed a ton, and Peggy asked if they could call her a taxi; walking back to the convention center would be an impossibility. Not only did they call her a cab, but they put the box on a little hand truck and called one of the younger assistants to haul it out to the curb for her.

'You know anything about this old guy, Miller?' Peggy asked as they went up the main aisle.

'He was a bit of a loon, I know – least that's what my uncle told me.'

'Your uncle?'

'Bert. He's one of the barmen at the Hole in the Wall.'

'Why did your uncle Bert think he was crazy?'

'He was forever getting newspapers, not proper English ones but foreign – the *El Observadorio* or something. And *A Voxey da Serra*, sounded like.'

'Interesting,' said Peggy. They reached the roll-up doors and went out into the sunlight. The dark man who'd sat beside her briefly in the auction room was smoking a cigarette, leaning on the rear fender of the Jag. He watched silently as the young assistant tipped the box off the hand truck and eased it on to the pavement.

'There you go, missus,' said the assistant.

She took a heavy one-pound coin and pressed it into the young man's hand. He handed it back. 'Not necessary, missus, but thank you all the same.' The young man smiled at her and headed back inside the auction hall. Peggy smiled back; it was the most politeness she'd received from a stranger since she'd done a photo essay for *The New York Times Magazine* on the Amish.

'How much did you pay for the box?' asked the man leaning on the Jaguar. The accent was cultured, but definitely eastern European. At a guess she'd have thought Russian, or maybe Czech. Whatever the accent, she didn't like the tone.

'Why do you care?' Peggy responded.

'It should have been mine.'

'You weren't there to bid on it.'

'A call of nature,' said the man.

'Well, I can't help that,' said Peggy. She looked up the street, wishing the taxi would come.

'The box should have been mine,' the man repeated, a little more insistently.

'You mentioned that,' said Peggy.

'I will pay you for it,' said the man.

'I'm not selling it.'

'I will give you a hundred pounds for it. You will make a profit.'

'I don't want a profit,' said Peggy, irritated. 'I want

the box and it's not for sale.' Why the hell did the guy with the Jaguar want a footlocker from 1928?

The taxi arrived, a boxy red Renault minivan with PRICE FIRST TAXI on the sliding door. The driver got out, opened the sliding door and hauled the footlocker inside. The man leaning on the Jaguar stepped forward and handed Peggy a business card.

'If you change your mind,' said the man. 'My cell phone number is there. Anytime, day or night. I will await your call.' The last bit had a slightly sinister edge to it, as though something bad would happen if the call didn't come.

'Don't lose any sleep waiting,' Peggy said. She took the card and got into the cab.

'Where to, missus?' the cabbie asked.

'Palace Hotel, please,' said Peggy.

'Right you are, missus.' The cab moved off.

Peggy looked at the card:

Dimitri Antonin Rogov
Expeditions
'Custos Thesauri'

'Custos thesauri?' Rafi Wanounou laughed, staring at the card Peggy had handed him. 'That's ripe coming from a man like Dimitri Rogov! *Latro thesauri* would be more like it.' They sat at the breakfast table in their

room at the Palace Hotel, the rusty footlocker between them.

'So what does it mean? Who is he?' Peggy asked her archaeologist husband.

'*Custos thesauri* means keeper, or guardian of the treasure, in Latin. *Latro thesauri* is the opposite, the thief of treasures. Dimitri Rogov would make Lara Croft look like an amateur and your beloved Indiana Jones a bumbling boob.'

'How dare you cast aspersions on my secret love!' Peggy laughed. 'You should look so good in a beat-up fedora.'

'You're sounding more like my mother every day,' said Rafi, smiling back. The truth was, of course, that when Rafi had brought a girl home named Peggy Blackstock, she hadn't been impressed. He told her the name in Yiddish was Schwarzekuh, but that didn't seem to help much, either.

'Seriously, though,' said Rafi. 'Rogov is infamous. He's a tomb robber, a smuggler, a forger and an all-round thief. If he wants something he'll do just about anything to get it.'

'Well,' said Peggy, 'maybe we should find out what's inside.'

It took the better part of an hour. A hammer and chisel borrowed from hotel maintenance, as well as spraying around the edges of the lid with something called Cillit Bang that came in a bottle with a bright pink label, finally did the trick.

The first thing out of the footlocker was the bundle of very frail-looking pinkish notebooks with faded designs on the covers. Rafi gently cut and removed the string; then, putting on a pair of the latex gloves he carried with him everywhere, he carefully opened the top notebook.

'*Benn-zonna!*' Rafi swore, his eyes widening as he stared down at the words in faint, sepia-colored ink.

Being the Private Journals of
Lt Col. (R.A.) Percival Harrison Fawcett
in Search of the Lost City of Z

'I think it's time we gave your cousin a call,' said Rafi slowly. 'I think we're going to need him.'

2

'It is a bug,' said Eddie Cabrera, staring down at the thing in the box. 'A very big bug, but still a bug after all.'

'But don't you see? It can't be a bug.'

'It is a bug.' Eddie shrugged. 'It has wings and many little feet and a round head with antennae sticking out of it. Of course it is a bug, my friend. It can be nothing else.'

'What I mean is it can't be a bug in the present. A creature this large only got that way because of the much heavier concentrations of oxygen in the air millions of years ago.'

'All right, then,' said Eddie. 'It is a very old bug.'

'But it's not,' said Rafi. 'It's only been dead for a few years, a hundred at most.'

'A dead bug is a dead bug, Doctor. How long it has been dead and pinned down to a piece of wood with its wings torn off is of very little interest to the bug in question. A hundred years, millions, what does it matter to the bug?'

'A philosophical Cuban, dear God,' murmured Rafi Wanounou.

'He's been hanging around with Doc for too long,' said Peggy Blackstock, sprawled across the couch in their suite at Claridge's Hotel in London and reading the room service menu. 'I wonder if I should have the chocolate and blackcurrant cannelloni or the praline streusel with the salt butterscotch ice cream.'

'How about a cup of tea with lemon and a slice of dry toast?' said Rafi.

'Is that supposed to be a comment on my weight?' Peggy asked. 'Because we haven't been married long enough for you to make comments like that.'

'It's a comment on the health of your arteries,' laughed Rafi. 'I am a doctor, you know.'

'You're a doctor of archaeology,' said Peggy. 'The last artery you looked at belonged to a ten-thousand-year-old mummified dog.'

'It was a cat actually.'

Lieutenant Colonel John 'Doc' Holliday, U.S. Army Rangers (retired), came out of one of the bedrooms in the lavish hotel suite, a stapled folder in his hands containing a photocopy of the complete journals Peggy and Rafi had found in the chest picked up at the auction in Torquay. 'Has anyone actually read these things?' he asked.

'I flipped through them,' said Peggy with a shrug.

'I thought I'd leave that to you,' said Rafi.

'Fawcett made eight trips to the Amazon Basin. On the last one he disappeared.'

'Which is when all the legends started.' Peggy nodded.

'Two things that are mentioned in the journals – he was financed by a mysterious group that called itself "the Glove" and he made a secret trip to the Arquivo Distrital de Lisboa, the Lisbon Archives in Portugal. He was particularly interested in a shipping company owned by someone named Pedro de Menezes Porto-carrero, a high-ranking officer in the navy and also a big wheel in the spice trade, particularly pepper, which was worth its weight in gold back in the four-teen hundreds. It also appears that Pedro was a bigwig in the Real Ordem dos Cavaleiros de Nosso Senhor Jesus Cristo.'

'The Templars,' said Eddie. 'The same as the Brotherhood in Cuba.'

'Exactly,' said Holliday. 'Anyway, in 1437 he sent three of his biggest ships to Goa in the Indian Ocean. They were the *Santo Antonio de Padua*, the *Santo Ovidio de Braga* and the *Santo João de Deus*. He also dropped off a man in the Azores named Gonçalo Velho Cabral, a Portuguese monk and commander in the Order of Christ who was effectively the first governor of the islands. Cabral was traveling on board the *Santo Antonio de Padua* and mentioned to the captain that the ship seemed to be riding very low in the water for a vessel under ballast and outward bound in search of cargo.'

'Too much information, too many names,' complained Peggy.

'Give me a second,' soothed Holliday. 'I'm getting to the point.'

'Thank God,' muttered Peggy.

'After voicing his suspicions the captain simply handed Cabral a white leather glove and nothing more was said. Fawcett only discovered this by cross-indexing Cabral's name in the archives and reading his journals. The glove was a sign that the ships were on Templar business, so Cabral kept his mouth shut.'

'Go on,' said Rafi, taking an interest now, his enormous, impossible 'bug' forgotten for the moment.

'Back then riding currents was really the only way to navigate. For a ship to go from Lisbon to Goa, they'd ride the North Atlantic Drift down past the Canaries, catch the Equatorial Countercurrent under the Horn of Africa and then head west and south on the South Equatorial Current until they reached the Cape of Good Hope, where they'd swing east again and pick up the currents in the Indian Ocean. Except they never made it.'

'What does that have to do with Fawcett?' Peggy asked.

'Nothing,' said Holliday. 'Except that the South Equatorial Current swings right past the mouth of the Amazon, and while Eddie and I were cooling our jets in the Bahamas a while back, the Excalibur Marine

Exploration Corporation, which is a fancy name for a bunch of Brit treasure hunters, announced that they'd found the remains of a four-masted ship; there's almost no doubt that she's the *Santo Antonio de Padua.*'

'I still don't get it,' said Peggy. 'Boats sink or go down in hurricanes.'

'The ships were supposedly heading to Goa to pick up a shipment of pepper. According to Excalibur Marine Exploration, the hull of the *Santo Antonio de Padua* was stacked with barrels full of gold coins.'

'Coins to buy the pepper with.' Peggy shrugged.

'Twelve tons of French Charles the Fifth gold francs?'

'It does seem a bit extreme,' the young woman agreed.

'None of the ships ever made it to Goa and none of the ships ever returned.'

'You're saying they went up the Amazon?' Rafi asked.

'That, and something else; I think our friends "the Glove" knew that long before they financed Fawcett's trip.'

'*No entiendo,*' said Eddie. 'Explain this.'

'Sure. The guy who was the British grand master of the White Templars in 1925 was a man named Sir Hugo Sinclair, second viscount of Stonehurst and later Lord Grayle of Ashford.'

'We know this how?' Peggy asked.

'Because his name is in the notebook Brother Rodrigues gave me as he lay dying on the island of Corvo in the Azores. The same notebook that gave me the numbers I can use to pay for suites like this at Claridge's.'

'I thought you only used that money when it had something to do with the Templars now,' said Rafi.

'It does,' said Holliday. 'Guess who the chairman and CEO of Excalibur Marine is.'

'Tell us before we all die of curiosity,' sighed Peggy.

'Lord Adrian Grayle, Hugo Sinclair's grandson. One of the men on his board of directors is none other than Dimitri Antonin Rogov.'

'Oh dear,' said Peggy.

3

The British Museum of Natural History on London's Cromwell Road would have provided excellent lodgings for Harry Potter's Voldemort or Tolkien's Sauron. It had ten times more Victorian towers and oddball staircases than the Smithsonian Castle in Washington and looked even more ominous than the Spasskaya Tower in the Kremlin. All of which was a little odd since it was designed and built by a British Quaker named Alfred Waterhouse in 1881 – though perhaps not so odd given that Waterhouse's first commission as an architect had been a cemetery. The collections of the museum went back more than two hundred years to the 'Curiosities' collected by Sir Hans Sloane, the Irish physician, which eventually formed the basis of the British Museum, of which the Natural History Museum was an offshoot.

Rafi and the rest of the crew found Professor Kenneth Anger, Oxon, Balliol College, M.A., Ph.D. several times over, emeritus director of the Department of Invertebrate Anthropology in the tower room he'd been assigned to after turning seventy and stepping down as the active director. Anger himself looked like everyone's idea of a cartoon Merlin the Magician. He was barely more than five feet tall with long snow-white hair, a long white beard and wire-rimmed spectacles perched halfway down a Roman nose far too big for his plump, small face.

The professor's round office was relatively roomy and contained dozens of heavy shelves filled with bits and pieces of fossilized creatures, most of them insects. The leftover space was given over to a desk, piles of books and papers, three cozy armchairs upholstered in green leather and a gas fireplace in the corner. When they opened the door to the office, the diminutive professor was standing on the top rung of a rickety-looking wooden library ladder trying to find something on one of the upper shelves. He suddenly gave a cry of triumph, grabbed at a foot-square oblong of rock and proceeded to tip over backward, toppling off the ladder.

'*Dios!*' Eddie said. He took three huge steps forward and caught Anger only a split second from the stone floor and a fractured spine.

'Good Lord!' Anger said as Eddie stood him on his feet. He staggered weakly to his desk and sat down behind it. 'Very kind of you. I do hope you didn't strain anything.'

'You don't weigh much more than a bird, Professor.' Eddie smiled, towering over the man.

'*Qué tipo de ave?*' Anger asked curiously. The professor spoke eight different languages, the result of a lifetime spent digging up fossils all over the world.

'A large goose perhaps.' Eddie smiled again.

'Ah yes, *Anatidae*; quite a large family. Not my field really. There was a very large gooselike creature called *Dasornus emuinus*, which used to fly up and down the Thames fifty million years ago skimming the water for fish. It had teeth and a five-meter wingspan.'

'Fascinating,' said Rafi, sitting down in one of the armchairs. 'What would you call a meat-eating dragonfly with meter-long wings?'

'*Meganeura,*' said Anger promptly. 'I've got one or two in my collection.' He waved a small hand at the shelves around him.

'We've got one, too,' said Holliday. 'From a survivor of Fawcett's last expedition in 1925.'

'You can't mean Percy Fawcett,' said Anger.

'The very one,' replied Holliday.

'I had no idea he was interested in fossils,' said Anger musingly. 'I should have thought blowguns and shrunken heads would be more his sort of thing.'

'Apparently not,' said Holliday.

'You wouldn't happen to have brought it with you, I suppose.'

'As a matter of fact, we did,' said Peggy. She stood up, walked over to the professor's desk and put the box down in front of Anger. The elderly paleontologist took the top off the box and stared down into it.

'This can't be,' he said, looking up at his visitors, eyes blinking rapidly behind his spectacles.

'But it is,' said Rafi.

'But it can't be,' said Anger. 'It's scientifically impossible. During the carboniferous era a hundred million years ago, the atmosphere was much denser and the oxygen levels were extremely high. That's most of the reason creatures like *Meganeura* and *Dasornus emuinus* grew so large. The weight of their bodies and wings today would make it physically impossible to fly.'

'But it did fly, and not ten million years ago. The evidence is right in front of your eyes.'

'Is there any documentation regarding this ... insect's provenance?' Professor Anger asked, looking down into the box.

'None,' said Holliday.

'This doesn't require Sherlock Holmes to deduce,' said the professor. 'Fawcett explored the Amazon Basin primarily. We can assume that it came from somewhere in that vicinity.' Anger steepled his hands together under his very large nose.

'Big vicinity,' said Holliday.

'Not when you take the other necessary requirements into consideration.'

'An area of high oxygenation,' said Rafi.

'And somewhere isolated from the surrounding

ecosystems,' said the professor. 'A creature like this one wouldn't survive long in an area where there were large predators.'

'Where do you get areas of high oxygenation in the Amazon?' Peggy asked.

'The landform would most likely be a sinkhole of some sort, a large one,' said the professor. 'And it would require a great deal of nitre in the soil.'

'I was no good at high school chemistry,' said Peggy.

'*Salitre*,' said Eddie. 'In English you call it saltpeter.' He smiled. 'That Cuban education of mine, senora, it was very good no matter what you think of poor old Fidel.'

'Bravo, Senor Cabrera, quite right.' Anger nodded.

'So, where do you find that combination?' Peggy asked.

'A *tepui*, I should think, probably a large unexplored one next to the border with Venezuela.'

'Okay,' said Holliday. 'You've been a great help.'

'My pleasure,' said Anger. 'If there's anything else I can do to help . . .'

'Actually, there is,' said Holliday. 'You could take care of our *Meganeura* for us.'

'Certainly,' said the professor, 'I'd be happy to.'

'And keep it under your hat?'

'Under my hat . . . oh, yes, quite! Mum's the word.'

*

Pierre Ducos, French master of the White Templars, sat at the end of the long walnut table in the principal dining room of Lord Grayle's Stonehurst Hall, a long white leather gauntlet set formally in front of him.

Four other masters of the White Glove sat at the table with him: Lord Adrian Grayle, the third duke of Stonehurst, the English master; Klaus Tancred of Germany; Antonio Ruffino of Italy; and Katherine Sinclair of the United States, a distant cousin of Sir Adrian's. There was a gauntlet in front of each master, a tradition dating back to the original Templars and later adopted by the Masons, the white standing for purity, the jousting glove expressive of their willingness to take up arms for the cause.

'Can this man Rogov be trusted?' asked Ruffino, the rotund Armani-suited Italian.

'Of course not,' said Ducos. 'But his evidence can.' Ducos picked up his worn leather dispatch case and put it on the table. He withdrew a heavy object swathed in a covering of black velvet, then opened the cloth. Gleaming on the cloth was an oblong ingot of gold eight inches long, three inches wide and an inch thick. Stamped crudely in the center of the ingot was a Templar Cross. 'There is no doubt this comes from one of our three ships. From Rogov's data, it was most likely the *Santo Antonio de Padua*, the smallest of the three.'

'The other two reached their destination?' Sir Adrian asked.

29

'According to Rogov, there is no sign of either the *Santo Ovidio de Braga* or the *Santo João de Deus* at the wreck sight. Both ships had a shallow enough draft to reach far up the Amazon, and both carried barges to get even farther. According to Mrs Sinclair's connections with American remote sensing satellite corporations, there is evidence that both ships did reach the Lost City.'

'So let us go and retrieve what is ours.' Tancred the German master shrugged. 'What is the problem? Frau Sinclair certainly has the resources in the area, and funding is certainly not a problem.'

'The problem, I am afraid, is a dead monk named Helder Rodriguez and the potential involvement of his chosen acolyte, Lieutenant Colonel John Holliday.'

'This man Holliday, he haunts us at every step,' said Tacred bitterly.

'He has cost us a great deal of money, certainly,' said Ruffino.

'He cost me a daughter and a son,' said Kate Sinclair. 'I want him dead.'

'We all share your pain, Madame Sinclair, and also your desire to see him dead. The question is, how do we accomplish such a goal?'

'Perhaps my brother the cardinal can help us there.' Ruffino smiled, folding his hands across his ample belly.

*

In 1959, at the age of sixteen, Arturo Bonnifacio Ruffino, second son of Angelo Ruffino, one of the largest shoe manufacturers in Italy, made a momentous decision. He knew well enough that while he would have all the wealth he could ever desire, his brother, Antonio, would inherit the company now controlled by his father and, with it, the power.

Although he didn't have a religious bone in his body, Arturo knew that the next best place for him to gain the power, the desire for which was a constant need more addictive than any drug, almost certainly lay in the Church. With that in mind he enrolled in the archiepiscopal seminary of Milan that eventually and inevitably led him toward the Vatican.

The inevitability of his destination was predictable; his father was already a good friend to the Church, and after his son was ordained that friendship became even stronger. By twenty-five Ruffino was secretary to a bishop, and by thirty-five he was a bishop himself, active on more than one powerful committee. By fifty he was Holy See representative for the Vatican at the United Nations.

By fifty-eight he was elevated to cardinal and on the recent death of Cardinal Spada he was made the Vatican secretary of state. With the present Holy Father clearly ailing, there was only one final rung on the ladder. Along with the secretariat came the reins of Sodalitium Pianum, the Vatican Secret Service, its

31

longtime director, Father Thomas Brennan, recently gone to his heavenly reward in less than godly circumstances in the middle of an at-home massage given by a therapist who also happened to be an assassin. His choice to replace Brennan was a priest named Vittorio Monti, a friend from his first days at the seminary and also his longtime sexual partner.

Like Spada and Brennan before them, the two men rarely had confidential conversations in either man's office. During his first few months as director of Sodalitium Pianum, Monti, acting on Ruffino's instructions, had tapped every important phone line and bugged every important office and conference room in the Vatican with an assortment of high-tech audio and video devices. The walls of the Holy See really did have eyes and ears.

For totally private discussions the two men generally met early each day for prayer in the Sistine Chapel, four of Monti's men scattered around the church to ensure that no one except Michelangelo's God and all His saints were there to overhear them.

'My brother has a request,' said the cardinal.

'About this man Holliday you mentioned to me?' Monti asked.

'Yes,' said Ruffino. 'We've had a watcher on him since Brennan's time. He also wants you to keep a close eye on Sir Adrian Grayle.'

'And who is Grayle?'

'A British industrialist who does a great deal of business in Brazil. My brother is financially involved with him. He has heard rumors that Grayle is up to no good.'

The Secret Service director was not an ugly man, but he had a permanent and ungainly limp from a bout of childhood polio. Entering the seminary a year behind Ruffino, the slightly older boy had immediately taken the crippled and very self-conscious Monti under his wing. It was this early bond that had cemented Monti's loyalty to Ruffino and made him totally trustworthy.

'Where is Holliday now?'

'London, with his cousin, her husband and his friend, a Cuban named Cabrera. Grayle is in America, but he'll be back in London tomorrow.'

'The cousin recently discovered a number of potentially valuable notebooks. We need the notebooks and we need Holliday and his little entourage removed as a threat.'

'I'll get on it immediately.' Monti laid a small, smooth hand over the cardinal's. 'Tonight, Arturo? It has been too long already.'

'We'll see, Vittorio. I have a great deal of work to do.'

'I suppose you're right. I have work to do myself. I have to see Garibaldi.'

'Who is he?' Ruffino asked.

'You don't want to know. There is still such a thing as plausible deniability.'

'In a Church built on lies and betrayal? The Vatican has less plausible deniability than Richard Nixon ever did.'

'All right. Garibaldi is a member of the Assassini.'

'Good God, I didn't think they still existed,' said the cardinal.

'There aren't very many.'

'They are truly assassins still?'

'More like field operatives.'

'Vatican James Bonds?'

'I suppose you could call them that.'

'With licenses to kill.'

'If it comes to that.'

4

They made their way to Manaus from Heathrow in grueling hops with stopovers in Washington, D.C., Houston, Texas, and Caracas, Venezuela. By the time they reached the Park Suites Hotel in Manaus, a little more than twenty-four hours had passed. They all managed to shower, then stagger into bed, and that was that for their first day in Brazil.

The next morning, Holliday and the rest of the still-groggy crew made their way to the Alpaba Restaurant, the hotel's attempt at haute cuisine with a view out over the Rio Negro.

'It's kind of hard to concentrate on eggs Benedict when you're looking out at a river full of things big enough to swallow you whole or rip the flesh off your bones,' Peggy said.

'It's not that bad,' said Holliday. 'All that stuff about vampire fish swimming up your genital tract and sticking there is a lot of bunkum.'

'You shouldn't be eating hollandaise anyway.' Rafi grinned. 'It's not good for you.'

'Is that another comment about my weight?' Peggy bristled.

'I'm just teasing,' answered her husband. 'You haven't gained an ounce since Doc and I rescued you from those Tuareg bandits.'

'Took you long enough,' said Peggy, grumbling. 'And there are monster snakes out there. I saw it on the Discovery Channel.'

'We've got more than monster fish to worry about,' Holliday said.

'He's right.' Rafi nodded. 'If Rogov's not here, he soon will be.'

'This man, he is so dangerous?' Eddie asked.

'He usually travels with a bunch of Turkish and Syrian thugs – tomb robbers most of them. Hard men.'

'How would they get passports or visas to get into Brazil?' Peggy said.

'Not hard with Grayle and his people behind him,' Holliday said.

'Why would they come here?' Rafi asked. 'I thought all the stories about Fawcett have him traveling down the Xingu River on his last expedition.'

'Grayle's no fool,' said Holliday. 'The Xingu is famous for its rapids. Most of it's too shallow for even the *Santo Ovidio de Braga* or the *Santo João de Deus*. If he's following the ships, he'd follow the Amazon, and the Rio Negro is a "blackwater river" – deep and calm, more than deep enough for those shallow-draft ships. Not to mention the fact that Grayle's people may already be on our trail. Rogov wasn't trying to get that chest for no reason.'

'So what is our next move, amigo?' Eddie asked.

'We find a way to get up the Rio Negro to an ancient little place called Barcelos.'

They reached Barcelos aboard a Piper Comanche of indeterminate years, the pilot and copilot apparently flying using a photocopied map they had taped to the windshield. Below them was a solid carpet of dense rainforest broken only by the wide black line of the Rio Negro as it snaked its way northward. There wasn't a road to be seen.

Two hours later, after a remarkably smooth ride, they landed at Barcelos Airport, which seemed to be quite busy. There were even a few executive jets parked on the hardstands outside several hangars. A minibus was pulled up beside a Hawker 4000 and taking on passengers, all of them carrying long tubes. The sign painted on the minibus said RIO NEGRO FISHING TOURS. The name on the side of the jet was White Horse Resources.

'British,' said Holliday.

'A long way to come for a fish,' grunted Eddie.

'More money than brains,' agreed Peggy.

'*Y que lo digas,*' said Eddie.

'What?'

'You can say that again,' translated Holliday. 'White Horse is one of Grayle's companies.'

Their taxi this time was a sagging Ford Taurus driven by a giant sausage of a man with a few tufts of gray hair over his ears and the gurgling wheeze of someone with end-stage emphysema. He managed to get them to their destination, a three-storey hotel called Rio Negro that looked as though it had once been a nineteenth-century warehouse with a residence above it. The building was within a block or two of the Porto Velho, the Old Harbor.

The manager of the hotel, who gave his name as Mr Carlos, also seemed to be the maître d' of the family-style dining room, and while an aging bellboy took their luggage to their rooms Mr Carlos sat them at a table covered with a gingham tablecloth and a real candle in an empty bottle of port.

They had a pleasant enough meal of *cordonizes*, which was supposed to be quail but looked suspiciously like pigeon, served with an odd combination of rice and french fries, followed by something called *manjar branco*, a coconut pudding that was served with a sauce of pitted prunes poached in port wine. They finished off the meal with coffee.

'Pigeons, pudding, prunes and port,' said Peggy. 'A completely alliterative meal.'

'So, what's the plan?' Rafi asked. 'Rent a boat of some kind?'

'The last bit of civilization Fawcett mentioned in the journal is a town called São João Joaquin. It's at the junction of the Rio Negro and the Rio Icana, which flows up into Venezuela. This São João place was Fawcett's jumping-off place for heading into the jungle. It's about two hundred miles upstream.'

'No roads?' Rafi said.

'Nope,' said Holliday.

'Riverboat?' Eddie asked.

'There are a few, but even Fawcett didn't take one.'

'He flew?' Peggy said.

'He flew.'

His name was Yachay of the Hupda Indians and he was shaman of his village in the forest. Of his particular branch of the tribe, there were less than could be counted on the hands of ten men left. Once, a long time ago, there had been many, many more, but the traders and the missionaries had killed them with their spirit sicknesses and his village had moved ever deeper into the jungle that was their home. Still, there was danger and this time Yachay feared it would not come from any spirit sickness; it would come from the great gray monster that drank at their rivers.

He was old, although he didn't know how old. He

had fought a hundred battles and won most of them, lost sons and wives and nephews and untold friends. Now his only solace was in the taking of the *ipadu abiu* and the powder of the *xhenhet* and the visions they brought him and which he used to guide his people. He had taken the paste of the *ipadu* before beginning his journey, and it had foretold great danger.

His bare feet sank into the rich earth, and in his way he had become part of the forest and not an intruder in it. He could hear the crackling of dead leaves as the beetles foraged and the sound of the birds and monkeys and other creatures in the canopy above him. He could taste the drying air in his mouth and knew by the sun on his back how far he had come and how far there still was to go. He was as sure of this as his taking of breath and just as sure, some-how, that he would not let the monster kill his people.

The headquarters of the Pallas Group is located in McLean, Virginia, in a complex of buildings just off the George Washington Parkway and is surrounded by forestland on all sides. From his penthouse office on the twenty-eighth floor of the main building, Charles Peace, the CEO of Pallas, could see the headquarters for the Anti Terrorism Center, the CIA, the Pentagon and the Capitol building – virtually all the elements that made the Pallas Group tick.

Along the only wall in his office that wasn't made of glass, there were seven violins encased in glass and kept in perfect humidified and temperature-controlled conditions. In his collection there was a Guarneri, a Maggini, a Gasparo di Salò, an Amati e Bergonzi and two Stradivariuses. In monetary terms the collection was worth between seventy-five and a hundred million dollars, but in actuality the violins were priceless. At one time or another, Peace had played all of them. It was a favorite expression of his that generals and politicians were like the strings on a great violin: stroke them well and they would make beautiful music for you.

Sir Adrian Grayle, a gray-haired man in his mid-fifties, stared out at the stunning view from the penthouse office window, then turned back to Peace.

'In the very center of power, I see,' said Grayle, coming back to the comfortable armchair in front of Charles Peace, who was seated behind his massive desk. The desk had originally been used by F.D.R. in the Oval Office and a number of presidents who came after him. It had cost Peace a fortune.

'Being at the center of power is a requirement of the business,' answered Peace, 'and I like to see my enemies coming.' Peace was older than Grayle, with dark hair in a widow's peak. A pair of neon red half-frame bifocals was perched on the end of his nose.

'As I told you on the telephone, Mrs Sinclair suggested that I see you before I returned to England about helping to solve my current problem.'

'Yes, she mentioned you'd be calling.' Peace smiled thinly. 'What exactly is your problem?'

'I assume you know I'm the chairman of White Horse Resources, and I'm sure you also know that we have invested several billion dollars in the Itaqui Dam Project in northern Brazil.'

'I know something about the project. I understand you're having problems with the locals.'

'Forty-eight hundred assorted Hupda Indians and a territory that has recently been internationally recognized as a nature conservancy and also as a reserve for the Hupdas.'

'How does the Brazilian government feel about these people?'

'Noncommittal. They'd like to see them go away as much as I would.'

'We could probably arrange something,' said Peace.

'It can't be something as overt as President Belaúnde napalming the Matsés in Peru back in the Sixties,' Grayle cautioned. 'That would sink the Itaqui Project on the spot. The whole world can look over your shoulder these days.'

'In which case you show them something acceptable,' said Peace calmly.

'I'm not sure I understand,' said Grayle.

'Pallas controls a company called Firebreakers. It provides water bombers to countries all over the world as well as domestically. It owns one hundred and twenty Canadair CL-215 aircraft.'

'What does this have to do with my problem?'

'Twenty of those aircraft are held in reserve for the aviation arm of our security division. Those twenty aircraft have been retrofitted to drop something other than water.'

'Such as?' Sir Adrian asked.

'The quickest and most effective you have already mentioned – napalm – but the aircraft can also be fitted with tanks of liquid cow manure infected with *E. coli* O157: H7, an enterohemorrhagic strain. The manure would be dropped into the water supply, whatever river the group was closest to. All their children would be dead within twelve days, as would any pregnant women. The entire village would be infected and most elders would die, as well.' Peace coughed lightly into a closed fist. 'If you're looking for a near one-hundred-per cent kill rate, there is always anthrax, of course.'

'Good Lord,' murmured Grayle.

'Well, Sir Adrian, which is it going to be?'

'I'll have to think on it for a bit, perhaps consult my board.'

'Take as long as you want, Sir Adrian, but you know the saying – time is money.'

'I'm well aware of the fact,' said Grayle. 'Speaking of which, how are things going with our other project?'

'Andromeda?'

'Yes.'

'We have the satellite imaging you requested. I thought that we could meet at the lab in St Gallen in a week or so to go over the lower-altitude scoops.'

'The initial experiments have been most encouraging,' said Grayle.

'I'm pleased,' said Peace. 'As a long-term income stream, it may replace everything. It will certainly change the face of medicine, not to mention war.'

'All right,' said Grayle. 'Have your people call me when you have the results and I'll arrange things with Neri from the bank.'

5

The floatplane had been drawn up on the muddy beach of the old port using a pair of heavy skids and a hand-cranked chain winch. The aircraft was large, single engined and high winged with a fuselage that appeared to be fabric stretched over some sort of interior skeleton or frame. It had obviously been painted a number of times and was now a mottled dappled green, slapped on in an amateurish camouflage pattern. The leading edge of the wings had clearly been patched in several places, and the lower halves of the floats were coated with some sort of fungus or algae.

'What on earth is that?' Peggy said, staring at the aircraft.

'Our ride,' said Holliday.

'You're kidding me,' said Rafi. 'It looks ancient.'

'Nineteen thirty-six,' said a voice from behind them.

The man standing behind them was medium height wearing a pair of greasy coveralls and wiping his hands off on a rag. His features were vaguely Asian mixed with something else and he had a long jet-black ponytail. On the bulging biceps showing below his T-shirt he had a U.S. Army Ranger DEATH BEFORE DISHONOR tattoo. He walked toward them, his right leg noticeably stiff.

'Peggy, Rafi, Eddie, this is my good friend Chang-Su Diaz.'

'Hi,' said the man with the ponytail.

'Diaz,' said Eddie. *'Hablas español?'*

'Sí.' Diaz nodded.

'Avión es bonita,' said Eddie.

'Gracias, senor. Eres un piloto?'

'Sí. Gracias a la Fuerza Aérea de Cuba.'

'Ah, Cuba,' said Diaz.

'Charlie Diaz was part of a special incursion group into Colombia that I was heading up back in the Nineties,' said Holliday. 'He can fly anything with wings or rotors. He's just about the only person who flies supplies up to the river tribes upstream. Doctors Without Borders use him a lot. Despite his looks he's a good man.'

'How did you lose the leg?' Peggy asked bluntly.

'Doc and I were having a sit-down with a man named Tito Valdez. He shot me under the desk with a Turkish Bullpup shotgun.'

'What happened to Tito Valdez?'

'Doc shot him in the face six times.'

'You can really fly with one leg?'

'During World War Two, there was a man named Douglas Bader who flew Spitfires after losing both legs. He played a pretty good game of golf to boot,' said Holliday. 'Now, enough history.' He turned to Diaz. 'Did you get everything I asked for?'

'All the practical stuff including the two inflatables you asked for, and the boat is waiting. Presumably Eddie can manage it.'

'*Qué tipo de barco?*' Eddie asked.

'*Un barco de rio,*' Diaz responded.

'*Grande?*'

'*Quince metros.*'

'*No hay problema.*' Eddie smiled.

'What about weapons?' Holliday asked.

'Everything you asked for. Forty-fives, Winchesters, a Weatherby, some Stoner POWs, two Heckler and Koch MSG-90s and one FN Maximi light machine gun.'

'Why do we need weapons?' Peggy asked, startled.

Holliday laughed. 'Because it's a jungle out there, Peg.'

The priest sat in his small office in the Vatican Railway Station, his computer humming quietly and a copy of *Debrett's Peerage* open on the desk beside it. According to Debrett's, Lord Adrian Grayle was a long-standing member of Booth's. The priest, a

47

fifty-eight-year-old man named Francisco Garibaldi, had also hacked in to the Brook's website and had discovered that one Lord Jonathon Gibbs, third Baron Vauxhall, now resided in South Africa and rarely came to the club although he still kept up his membership. Garibaldi went on to Google, found a recent photo of Vauxhall and printed it out. He picked up his telephone and dialed the special number in the Vatican Printing Office.

'This is Father Garibaldi. I'd like a full identification package on Lord Jonathon Gibbs.' The priest paused. 'Yes, a U.K. passport, as well, and also a membership card for Booth's Gentlemen's Club. Two days. Thank you.'

Garibaldi broke the connection, then hit the buttons again. 'Gino? Francisco. How is my father? Good, good. Look, Gino, I need a favor. I need you to find out the kind of playing cards they use at Booth's in London, then make up a deck in my prescription. Fast, two days maybe.' He waited, listening, and then smiled. '*Buono*, Gino. You are a good friend. Call me when they're ready and I'll meet you at Rosati's. Good, good, see you then. Give Papa my love.'

Hank Rand sat on the couch in the Oval Office with his boss, Harrison White, the director of the Central Intelligence Agency, seated beside him. Hank Rand was director of the National Resources Division, the most secret of the CIA's covert departments.

'I hope you're right about this, Hank,' said White, flipping through the brief they were about to hand to the president. 'You know how he hates that bitch, but I don't want him thinking we're ass-kissing.'

'It's from our team in Venezuela and it's rock solid, Harrison. One of the Pallas Group's subsidiaries is about to bomb the piss out of the Indians in northern Brazil. Another Pallas division is managing that big dam project in the region.'

'And another division provides contract security troops and VIP transport in Iraq and Afghanistan and have been since Bush and that bozo Cheney,' Rand responded. 'And the guy who sits behind that big desk over there would like nothing better than to boot their asses and put Kate Sinclair in jail. This is his chance.'

The president came in, slipped off his suit jacket, loosened his tie and dropped down into the high-backed chair behind the resolute desk. There was nothing on the desk except a telephone and a wooden box full of giveaway pins. On the windowsill to his right were a few family pictures, including his wedding portrait.

'Boy Scout Medal of Honor Award with Crossed Palms,' said the president, having just come from a photo op.

'What do you do to get that?' Harrison White asked.

'This twelve-year-old kid was walking back to his tent at a jamboree or whatever you call them and he found two little kids, Cubs, I suppose. It turned out these two kids had been chewing on some sort of house plant that paralyses your throat. He used two pieces of a ballpoint pen and a penknife to give them emergency tracheotomies.'

'Jesus!' White said.

'So now he wants to become a surgeon, I suppose.' Hank Rand smiled.

'Nope,' said the president. 'He wants to become a lawyer.'

'Why in hell would he do something like that?' White asked.

'Said he'd have a better shot at the Oval Office. Twelve years old, he's already after my job.' They all laughed briefly. The president leaned forward, hands clasped in front of him. 'So, what do my favorite spies have for me today?'

'Kate Sinclair on a skewer if we play our cards right.'

'Best news I've had today. Almost as good as Osama bin Laden shot full of holes. Now, that was something to see!' The president gave a sigh of contentment and leaned back in his chair, hands behind his head. 'Do tell, gentlemen.'

*

The jungle unrolled like a mottled green undulating carpet of forest beneath the wings of the old aircraft. Charlie Diaz flew the plane on a rock-steady course that followed the dark snaking river a few hundred feet below them.

Contrary to Peggy's fears, Charlie Diaz was a top-notch pilot and the old bush plane flew without a clatter or a bang. Holliday sat on one of four jump seats directly behind the cockpit, and Eddie had the copilot's chair. Between Eddie and Diaz on the dashboard was a plastic sign that said COPILOT'S CHECKLIST: DON'T TOUCH ANYTHING AND KEEP YOUR MOUTH SHUT. It was repeated in Spanish and Portuguese. Rafi and Peggy sat opposite, Peggy clutching the side of her seat white-knuckled. The rest of the cabin was stuffed with their gear.

'So, what do you think now, Peg?' yelled Holliday, raising his voice above the unmuffled monster outboard motor bellow of the engine.

'I think I'm going to puke,' she answered, her face white. 'He flies like he's operating a roller coaster.'

Rafi patted her knee consolingly. 'It's smooth as silk,' he said. 'It just *sounds* like we're going to crash any second.'

Right on cue the engine noise changed, and they went into a long, steep dive.

'Oh, crap!' Peggy screamed, gripping her seat even tighter.

'*No quieres intentar lo hacer aterrizar, mi amigo?*' Diaz asked Eddie, turning in his seat.

'*Con mucho gusto!*' Eddie replied.

'What are they saying?' Peggy asked. 'What are they saying? Are we going to crash?'

'Charlie just asked Eddie if he wanted to land the plane, and Eddie said sure,' translated Holliday.

'Shit,' Peggy said.

Eddie pulled back on the wheel of the Norseman and took a long, shallow run just above the water, looking for deadheads and other obstacles. Ahead of them and to the right was a series of rickety docks jutting out on to the smooth dark river, the jetties crammed with boats of all shapes and sizes. Whatever town existed here seemed to be higher up the steep bank of the river – roughly made plank buildings with thatched roofs.

'São João Joaquin, gentlemen,' said Diaz, pointing.

Eddie finally eased back on the throttle and simultaneously pulled back on the wheel, guiding them down on to the water, the long aluminum cutting neat wakes on either side of the fuselage. It was a perfect landing.

'*Muy bien.*' Diaz smiled.

'*Gracias,*' replied Eddie.

Diaz took over the controls and guided them toward one of the longest piers that jutted out into the river. Across from Holliday, Peggy's color was noticeably returning and her fingers had released their death clutch on the sides of her jump seat.

'There're boys who will transfer the gear on to the boat, but we must go up the bank to speak with Nanderu.'

'Who's Nanderu?' Peggy asked.

'The man who's going to guide us upriver,' said Holliday.

They clambered out of the plane and headed up the rickety pier. A swarm of young men dressed in kiltlike skirts crowded around the Norseman like baby birds around their mother. The leader was about twelve years old with skin the color of buckwheat honey. He was the only one of the crew giving orders and the only one wearing a Chicago Bulls T-shirt.

Diaz led the way up a steep flight of roughly made plank steps to the top of the riverbank. There were half a dozen plank buildings along the bank, some of them cantilevered over the slope. There seemed to be a small boatyard where at least a score of men in their kiltlike clothes were building narrow plank-on-frame boats, the planks joined with handmade rope and the seams sealed with a thick white tarry sap applied with strips of bark dipped into turtle-shell containers. The sap dried to a hard brown color that looked exactly like a heavy layer of varnish.

Diaz entered an open-sided thatch-roof establishment with half a dozen or so men drinking at tables and a makeshift bar. The beer of choice appeared to be a brand called Brahma.

Two men were sitting at a large round table on the far left. One was in his sixties, his long jet-black hair threaded with strands of white, his skin the color of a seamed and ancient oak. The man beside him was in his thirties with the same long black hair. His skin was a richly creamed coffee. Both men were high cheekboned and strong faced, their brown eyes large and intelligent. Neither man was drinking, but the younger man had a rifle in front of him on the table. It looked to Holliday like a Short Magazine Lee-Enfield Mk. 1, in use from the mid-1920s on and a staple of the British Army.

'This is Nenderu,' said Diaz, nodding toward the older man, 'and this is his grandson, Tanaki. Tanaki's English is quite good, so he will be your translator. He is also a fine hunter and tracker.'

'Tell your grandfather we are grateful for his help,' said Holliday.

The younger man turned to Nenderu and spoke briefly to him in Hupda.

The older man nodded formally at Holliday. 'My grandfather says he is glad to help,' said Tanaki. The grandfather spoke again and once again Tanaki translated. 'My grandfather says that we should get on the boat as quickly as possible. It is about to begin raining and it will be better to get under way before it does.'

'It's bright sunshine out there,' Peggy whispered to Holliday.

'It's his territory. We follow his advice,' he answered.

The heavy rain hissed against the thatch of Yachay's hut with a sound like the crackling of a fire. The *xhenhet* paste was in a stone bowl between his knees. *Xhenhet*'s botanical name was *Banisteriopsis caapi*, also known as *ayahuasca*, a potent psychotropic drug that had been informing Yachay's dreams and visions since he had first been selected as shaman at the age of thirteen.

Yachay leaned forward and scooped up the paste with two fingers, laying them across his tongue. He waited, humming quietly to himself, listening to the rain and staring at the two skulls on the altar. Both of the skulls had gold and silver teeth and both had eye sockets filled with the green stones the miners fought and killed for. The skull on the left had a talisman clutched between its upper and lower jaws. It was a round object of steel and glass that the man whose skull it was had valued highly for its magic. There was even a magic incantation written on the back that Yachay had pondered over many times. Three letters: PHW.

Yachay felt the *xhenhet* begin to take him and he sighed happily. Soon the skulls would talk to him and tell him what must be done.

6

The young woman ran through the rainforest jungle, her bare feet instinctively avoiding the pitfalls and dangers that lay in her path. Soon after they had taken her, they'd given her shoes and a bright red tank top and a short pink skirt to excite the men they brought to her, but once through the fence she'd shed everything, the colors of the clothing no better than a target on her back in a jungle where no such colors existed.

She ran to the west, searching for the river, for she knew that if she found the river she would find her way home. She was a Yuruti, daughter of a chief. Her name was Kachiri and she was sixteen years old.

What Kachiri was running from was an illegal diamond-mining facility, the exploitation of any mineral resource on an Indian reserve being strictly prohibited by law.

The location had initially been mined as an alluvial gold deposit, but deeper exploration had revealed a much deeper layer of so-called '*cascalho*' or diamondiferous-bearing rock. The open pit mine was now two hundred and eighty feet long, seventy feet across at its widest point and seventy-eight feet deep.

The entirety of the mine was covered by a steel girder, mesh and nylon camouflage net graciously provided by White Horse Resources, one of the major partners in the Itaqui Dam Project ninety miles or so to the north. The same camouflage covered the sorting buildings, the grading house, the office, the barracks and the brothel-bar nearby. A quarter of a mile to the south, there was a helicopter LZ used to ferry in shifts of the sorters, graders and security squads on a two-week rotation. The mine workers were given one day off in ten and worked twelve-hour shifts.

When not working they were required to stay within the compound fence, which was electrified. They were not allowed to hunt or forage and were forced to follow a high-protein diet of concentrated foods usually fed to the military when on active duty. There was a great deal of sickness among the workers, but as attrition lowered the labor force, more workers were brought in from outlying areas.

Since the horror show in Cuba the year before, the Pallas Group had wisely decided that the image of Blackhawk Security was permanently damaged and needed a major overhaul. The company was dissolved and out of its ashes was born White Star Protective Solutions, a name with a much lower profile and a benign image.

Of course in reality very little had changed beyond the shoulder patches and the letterhead. In an effort to keep that low profile, the rank indications on the operation camouflage of the White Star battle dress uniform bore no relation to the previous standard military markings. At White Star rank was shown by a strip of colored ribbon below the name. Green for a sergeant, blue for a lieutenant, red for a captain, white for a major, black for a colonel and silver for a general. It was all simple and unobtrusive.

The man tracking Kachiri was a captain named Thomas Plunkett, the direct descendant of Sergeant Thomas Plunkett, who had fought in the Battle of Waterloo against Napoleon Bonaparte.

Like the Thomas Plunkett of history, his present-day namesake was a master sniper, which had been his occupation in both Iraq and Afghanistan as well as several missions into Pakistan and more than a few jobs for Blackhawk Security.

In a number of emerging countries as well as some very ancient ones, not having an assassin in your Rolodex could be a serious flaw in your business plan. During slow times in corporate assassination, Plunkett was usually assigned to jobs like this: protection of high-value assets like the diamond mine and somewhat lower-value assets like Kachiri – valuable because of the services she performed and a major security risk should she reveal what she knew about the hidden and illegal mine.

Plunkett had been trailing Kachiri in the rain for half a day, following broken foliage, crushed undergrowth and muddy footprints through the jungle heading almost due west. She was making for the river and what she assumed was safety, but she was slowing and Plunkett knew he would catch her eventually. In some ways he was saddened by the inevitability of his success.

Like most of the people in this or any other jungle, she was not the master of her fate. The young women, some as young as twelve, had been gathered up by other Indian tribes and then sold to White Star, who in turn sold them to the company that owned the mine. When they were no longer of any value to the company, White Star paid the original raiding parties to dispose of them.

Plunkett spotted Kachiri in mid-afternoon. She had stopped under the shelter of a towering kapok tree, head bowed with exhaustion. Plunkett lifted his rifle. His weapon of choice was usually an Accuracy International AX 50, but today he was carrying a much lighter Dan-Inject projector rifle.

Putting his eye to the scope sight, Plunkett aimed for the base of the girl's neck and fired. There was a sharp cracking sound like a branch being snapped in two and then the girl slumped to one side.

Plunkett crossed the fifty feet separating them and squatted down beside the girl's motionless figure. He felt her wrist and quickly found a pulse. Pushing back her jet-black hair, he found the tranquilizer dart and removed it. He dropped the spent injector dart into a pouch at his side, then stood up, taking his radio out of its holster.

'I've got her. Come and get me,' he said. Back at the mine they would take his GPS location from the tracer in his pack and send out one of the eight-wheeled Mudd Ox ATVs they used for transportation. At speeds of up to twenty miles per hour, the journey that had taken him more than half a day would take the agile ATV less than a fifth of that time. He and the girl would be back in camp before dark. He sat beside her under the big kapok tree and settled down to wait.

Father Francisco Garibaldi, one of the last remaining Assassini and traveling under the passport of Lord Jonathon Gibbs, late of Cape Town, South Africa, entered Booth's Club on St James's Street in London, proffered his membership card at the registration desk and handed his overcoat to the uniformed porter.

After eating a meal of roast grouse and buck rabbit with British raspberries in crème fraîche for dessert in the dining room, he went up the broad main staircase to the games room, a large chamber with tall windows covered by heavy drapes and a ceiling of complicated plaster moldings.

He purchased twenty thousand pounds' worth of plaques from the cashier, then asked for directions to the vingt-et-un tables. There were three of them clustered at the far end of the room and closest to the bar. Grayle was at the closest one, a heavy crystal Scotch glass by his right hand and a cigarette in his left. The tables were semicircular with seating for six players.

Other than Grayle, there were two other men at the table. Garibaldi chose to sit on the far left. The dealer was using a card shoe with standard Cartamundi green-backed, plastic-covered playing cards exactly like the one in the left-hand pocket of his evening jacket.

He stayed out of the play for a few minutes watching the exquisitely dressed Grayle work the cards. Grayle was a man of roughly his own age, gray haired and slimly handsome with the arrogant, slightly aloof expression common to the English ruling class. His nails were perfectly manicured with just a hint of artificial gloss, his wedding ring was a simple gold band and the signet ring on his right index finger was the tower and helm crest of the Grayle family. The wristwatch was an Audemars Piguet Royal Oak Tourbillon in gold that looked as thin as a credit card.

Garibaldi watched Grayle play for a dozen hands, betting steadily but not enormously, splitting or doubling down when he had the chance and rarely taking risks. Grayle had no obvious tells like playing with his ring or blinking too much or running his hand through his hair, but this wasn't the kind of game where things were obvious. Garibaldi did notice a certain flaring of His Lordship's nostrils when he had two face cards or a perfect twenty-one, but that was about it.

He wasn't counting cards and he wasn't following any system that the priest could see; a man who gambled for recreation only and not because he was good at it or had it riding on his back like a demon.

Garibaldi began to play in much the same way but with slightly larger bets. When Grayle got bored and tossed a fifty pound plaque as a tip to the dealer, Garibaldi did the same.

'Stand you a drink in the bar, Lord Grayle?' Garibaldi said as they left the table. Garibaldi had always been something of a mimic, and his South African accent was nearly perfect.

'You know me?' Grayle asked.

'Only by reputation, Your Lordship, and we are in the same business.'

'Really?' Grayle said.

'Diamonds,' said the priest.

*

63

Holliday stood on the main deck of the SS *Amador* and stared out into the blinding sheets of rain that pockmarked the river in front of them. The rain was so heavy that the jungle on either side of the ancient sternwheeler was nothing but a dark green blur. Peggy and Rafi were crowded into the pilot-house above him while the two guides, Nenderu and Tanaki, squatted in the stern, protected from the rain by the deck overhang just like Holliday in the bow.

Even with the pounding rain and the steady chugging rumble of the paddlewheel, a strange silence had settled over everything, and Holliday found his thoughts wandering into strange places he hadn't been to in many years.

Another jungle many years ago and his night patrol was moving through the tangled ferns and grass and vines and mud when one of Charlie's tin pie plate versions of a Claymore went off at waist level, cutting Rusty Smart in half and sending body parts in all directions.

Rusty had been walking point and Holliday, a corporal then, had been two men back in the line. Rusty's left forearm, wrist and hand were there in the mud, all blood, shredded flesh and splintered bone, and on his wrist the Timex his dad had given him for graduating from high school. Rusty always had it set on

Chicago time, so it was reading seven thirty in the morning.

All Holliday could think of was that Rusty was dead but his watch was still telling time. 'Takes a licking but goes on ticking.' His dad would be sitting down to ham and eggs and home fries at Johnnie's Grill, and his son was dead and the Timex still worked. It was all there, but none of it fitted together.

And he remembered lying with Fay in her hospital bed that bright sun-filled morning, cradling her in his arms and then feeling the life come out of her in an instant like the crumpled beginnings of a love letter tossed on to the floor. Standing in the bow of the boat, he felt his tears begin to fall for her and for Rusty Smart, who hadn't been cried for in a very long time, and then he stepped forward out of the protection of the deck overhang and into the rain itself, feeling it hit his upturned face and eyes, the rain like tiny painful flecks of glass on his skin and his tears pouring for all those people he had loved and known and who had died and he felt his heart break into a thousand pieces and wondered if it would ever be whole again.

'He thinks sad thoughts, that one,' said Tanaki to his grandfather, both of them sitting in the shadows of the stern, their voices low and unheard below the shouting of the rain and the thunder of the paddlewheel.

'That is because he sees death ahead of him on the river,' replied Nenderu. 'Perhaps even his own.'

'And we lead him to this?' Tanaki asked.

The old man nodded. 'This our fate and his, as well, and this I think cannot be changed.'

7

The Mudd Ox from the mine arrived at Plunkett's GPS coordinates just before sunset, which didn't please the driver at all because he'd have to drive back in the dark and the nighttime jungle gave him the creeps. His name was Wally Beaman and he was here because he'd spent four years in Iraq and Afghanistan driving Humvees and lived to tell about it. The Mudd Ox was a long way down from a Humvee, but driving the ugly eight-wheeled ATV with the potbellied body paid three times as much.

Plunkett was sleeping under a kapok tree, but there was no sign of the girl. He'd probably underdosed her and when he was asleep she'd run off. Beaman grinned. Plunkett was never going to live this one down.

Beaman climbed out from behind the wheel of Mudd Ox and headed across the clearing to the kapok tree. He stopped dead, his hand going to the MP5 clipped to his Sam Browne. There were two four-inch darts sticking out of Plunkett's cheek, the end of each dart fletched with a wad of cotton like fiber from the seedpods of the same kind of tree Plunkett was lying under.

The darts were blowgun projectiles tipped with curare and used for hunting by the local Indians. They were usually only used on small birds and animals, but most tribes also maintained a supply of the toxin from the golden dart frog, a one-milligram dose of which is capable of killing a bull elephant. Plunkett would have been dead before he even felt the darts hit his cheek.

Beaman listened. As usual at this time of day, the jungle was like an orchestra tuning up before a performance. Tinamous and horned screamers fought it out with piping guans and pale-winged trumpeters. Military macaws tried to outdo platoons of blue-headed parrots, and howler monkeys tried to screech louder than anything. It was like the overture to a nightmare.

There was a faint rustling sound that was out of tune. He pulled the MP5 off its snap clips and raised it, but by then about a dozen Hupdas appeared out of the jungle, the upper part of their faces painted solid black, the lower blood-red.

'Shit,' Beaman said. He dropped the MP5 to the ground, but it was no good. The six men lifted their blowguns simultaneously and then Beaman knew exactly how quickly Plunkett had taken to die.

São João Joaquin, Fawcett's last-known contact with civilization, was located on the west bank of the

Negro River, but according to the journals the expedition actually began on the east bank at an unnamed village where he purchased canoes for his party and then bearers, seven boats in all.

The rain, which had ended only a few hours before, had raised the water level of the river substantially, and the rudimentary docking facilities on the east-bank side were almost inundated. Fortunately Eddie had just enough room to moor the old riverboat.

'Do you really think we'll find anything?' Peggy asked her husband as they tied up to the rickety dock.

'Trees and water,' laughed Rafi. 'Lots of trees, lots of water.'

They all disembarked and climbed the half-rotted steps up to the top of the bank. The village was a scattering of buildings, and most of the people squatting outside their entrances looked all or at least part Indian. Eddie began organizing porters to unload their gear and Tanaki approached Holliday.

'My grandfather says there is a man here who was one of Fawcett's luggage bearers on the last expedition. Would you like to see him?'

Holliday laughed. 'How old is this guy?'

'He was sixteen at the time. His name is Palala Santos. Half Indian and half Brazilian. He is very old and has no teeth, but his eyes are bright and his thoughts are clear. He has many things to say, according to my grandfather.'

'For how much?'

'He asks for tobacco only. He likes the small cigars, if there is a choice.'

They found Santos in something more than a hut but less than a shack at the edge of the village. A faint path led into the jungle beside the little structure, and howler monkeys played find-me, catch-me in the boughs of a strangler fig that stood a few feet away. Santos was squatting outside his hovel, a wide plank balanced on two plastic milk cartons in front of him. His face was a mass of wrinkles and creases and his once black hair was almost entirely white, but as Tanaki had said his dark eyes were clear, bright and intelligent. On the plank in front of him was a row of leathery shrunken heads. They looked very old, the skin almost black and as thin as parchment.

Peggy went white, her eyes wide. 'Those aren't real, are they?'

'Most Amazon tribes were once headhunters, but that was a very long time ago,' Tanaki said, his tone neutral.

'They're probably just howler monkeys for the tourists,' said Rafi.

'Howler monkeys have big canines,' said Holliday. 'These are real enough.'

Santos mumbled something to Tanaki and gave him a small skin bag from the pocket of his tattered, homemade shorts.

'He says the heads are from the time of the men who came here on cloud wings.'

'Cloud wings?' Peggy said.

Tanaki handed the skin bag to Holliday, who poured the contents into his hand: two gold Byzantine solidi, two Spanish gold doubloons and four gold Portuguese reais from the fifteenth century.

'Santos found it behind the sewn-up eye sockets of four of the heads,' said Tanaki.

'Sails,' said Holliday. 'The big sails on the *Santo Ovidio de Braga* and the *Santo João de Deus*, the other two ships of the flotilla sent out by Pedro de Menezes Portocarrero in 1437.'

'If they were like the ship they just found at the mouth of the Amazon, it means they were probably full of gold,' Rafi said.

'So the question is, what were two galleons doing bringing treasure to the middle of nowhere?'

Charles Peace, chairman of the Pallas Group, sat at a rear table at McKeever's Pub in McLean, Virginia, with his chief analyst, Cornell Desmond. Peace was having the filet mignon; Desmond was having the corned beef and cabbage. The pub was busy with the lunchtime crowd of low-level bureaucrats, and the place was noisy.

'I hope there's some reason for being here, Desmond; I must say I prefer the ambience and the menu in the executive dining room.'

'I know, sir, but I felt the situation required discretion.'

Desmond had the brain power of Harry Potter on a bad day. It had to be serious. 'What situation?'

'The Hupda.'

'What about them?'

'RAID-Three shows a large number of them heading north into the Itaqui reserve perimeter.'

RAID stood for Resource Access and Intelligence Device. Four of the satellites had been launched between 2005 and 2010 using Arianespace S.A., a private facility in France. The satellites were in geostationary orbit over a variety of 'hot spots' Pallas dealt with on a regular basis. Supposedly used for remote sensing of possible natural resources, they were actually equipped with the latest American 'Misty' technology and were as good as any surveillance satellite in space. RAID came courtesy of several American senators and congressmen who were sympathetic to their efforts.

'What's a large number?' Peace asked.

'At the moment it would appear to be something over two thousand.'

'Are they heading for the mine or the dam?'

'Neither, sir. They're heading almost due north into the deep jungle.'

'Shit,' Peace said. 'They're heading for Jurassic Park.'

'It would seem that way, sir,' said Desmond.

*

Cardinal Arturo Ruffino, Vatican secretary of state, walked through the gloomy vaulted stacks of the Vatican Library, his longtime friend and now head of the Holy See's Secret Service, Vittorio Monti, at his side.

'So, exactly what is this document you are about to show me?' Monti asked.

'One of the few documents in the Vatican Secret Archives that really is secret,' Ruffino said. 'And that's mostly because few men have ever had the wit to look for it.' Contrary to conspiracy theories and popular fiction, the Secret Archives are not temperature and humidity controlled or secured by laser beams in a vault buried deep beneath the Vatican. Contained in an annex to the Main Vatican Library, the archives are secret because they contain documents owned personally by the pope. The only men other than the Holy Father who have free access to the archives are the archive prefect and his minions. All others must ask for a particular volume or document, which will be brought to them in a reading room adjacent to the archive entrance.

They reached the Porta Angelica, passed through it to the Porta di Santa Anna and paused to show their credentials to the two Swiss Guards there. One of the archive prefects took them to a small reading room and locked them in. On the table in front of them was a box of surgical gloves and a large leather- and wood-bound volume, the Latin title still faintly legible in gold leaf on the cover:

Record of Ship Arrival and Departure Fees,
Port of Lisbon, 1347–1348

'Follow the money, Vittorio.' The cardinal smiled as he sat down at the table and snapped on a pair of the surgical gloves. 'Always follow the money.'

8

Eddie spent the next day and a half going up the Rio Negro, then swinging carefully on to the much narrower and much muddier Rio Xeruini. Both sides of the river were covered with dense jungle that reached the banks.

'According to Fawcett the river was full of fish,' said Holliday, standing on the bridge with Eddie as the SS *Amador* steamed slowly upriver heading north, the paddlewheel throwing up a brown-black wake of mud and ooze.

'Our Indian friends seemed to have discovered this already,' Eddie replied, nodding his chin down toward the main deck. Tanaki and Nenderu, his grandfather, were gutting an enormous fish that must have been six or seven feet long before the two men starting slicing it up.

'What the hell is it?' Holliday said.

'Tanaki said it's an arapaima,' answered Rafi, stepping through the bridge doorway carrying a string bag full of dripping cans of Caracu and Brahma beer. 'It's a living fossil. Nenderu says he's seen them ten feet long.'

'How did they catch it?'

'Tanaki speared it. He's says there's enough for every-one on board with leftovers for breakfast tomorrow.'

They stood, drinking beer and watching the muddy river and the jungle-choked banks moving slowly by.

Rafi took one of the volumes of the photocopied journals out of one of the innumerable pockets in his old Israeli Army fatigue jacket and flipped through it. 'This must be the greatest case of misdirection in history. All three of his previous expeditions went south, but the fourth one goes north even though everyone thinks she's going south again.'

'Initially I don't think it was misdirection. I think he found something else other than the three ships sent west full of treasure,' said Holliday, taking a healthy sip of the cold beer.

'Such as?'

'He went to three places to do his research: the maritime archives in Spain, the maritime archives in Portugal and the archives in Venice. Most of the ships built, purchased or leased were owned by the Zeno bothers, Antonio and Nicolo. The family had a monopoly on all ships going to the Holy Land.' Holliday took another hit from the can of beer. 'He made a notation on the flyleaf of the journal on the page where he describes his trip to Venice, on the Orient Express, no less. I still haven't figured it out.'

'What volume is it in?' Rafi asked.

'Two.'

'Give me five minutes,' said Rafi, and disappeared. He was back in four. 'Is this it?'

'That's the one,' said Holliday. He took the stapled photocopy from Rafi and flipped through the pages. 'There,' he said, pointing. The notation read:

P.D.A.TS 3/31

'What the hell is that supposed to mean?'

'Beats me.' Holliday shrugged.

'May I see it?' Eddie asked. Rafi handed it over to the Cuban, who read it and then laughed. 'No one noticed there was no period between *S* and *T*?'

'What difference would that make?' Rafi asked.

'Read the whole thing backward,' Eddie said. 'It is a children's code.'

'ST.A.D.P. 1373,' Rafi said after a few seconds. 'I still don't get it.'

'That is because you did not have a Catholic mother who dragged her youngest child to Mass even though Fidel forbid it.'

'Tell us, then.'

'San Antonio di Padua, patron saint of lost things, and my mother was always losing me because I was always running away.'

'A Templar ship in 1373? That's almost seventy years before the treasure ships left Portugal.'

77

'Was he famous for finding anything in particular?' Holliday asked.

Eddie nodded. 'Most often he is associated with the *Arca de la Alianza.*'

'The Ark of the Covenant,' whispered Rafi.

'*Sí*,' said Eddie.

'Holy shit,' said Rafi.

A red speck appeared directly in front of them almost at eye level. Holliday could hear the distant grinding roar of turboprop engines. 'A plane, flying low,' he said, squinting ahead. It slowly resolved itself into a high-winged, narrow flying boat. There was suddenly a series of twinkling lights on both wings.

'*No! No de nuevo!*' Eddie growled. He turned to Rafi. 'Take the wheel!'

Rafi did as he was told as Eddie turned and slammed open the door of the pilothouse cabin. He came out a few seconds later carrying the Stoner automatic rifle, the FN Maximi and two heavy belt ammunition boxes. He dropped the ammunition boxes out from under one arm and handed both weapons to Holliday. Eddie pushed up the trapdoor in the pilothouse roof and boosted himself through.

'It looks like a water bomber,' said Rafi as the blood-red aircraft approached.

'You see any forest fires?' Holliday asked. 'And when does a water bomber have machine guns in its wings?'

'What do I do?'

'Head for the shore. Try to run her aground.'

Eddie's strong black arm appeared through the trapdoor and Holliday handed him the weapons and the ammo boxes one by one, then followed them through the opening. He boosted himself up and took the Maximi from Eddie, who was gripping the automatic rifle. Directly ahead of them the red boat-hulled bomber was almost skimming the water, the double machine guns in each of the high-slung wings now chewing into the bow of the riverboat.

'She comes very low, this aircraft,' said Eddie, feeding a belt into the left-hand receiver of his weapon. Holliday did the same for the Maximi.

'The Canadair has a payload of about six tons. If it drops a load of water and muck directly on to us, it'll crush this old barge to matchsticks.'

'Then we must not allow this to happen, must we, *compadre*?' grunted Eddie, giving his friend a wink. 'Which part of this flying duck would you like to eat first, my friend?'

'I'll take the cockpit. You go for the props. Together maybe we can do some damage.'

'Sounds like a plan, boss.' Eddie grinned.

Holliday shook his head. 'Where do you get this stuff?'

'*Americana TV*, boss,' Eddie answered, then turned back to the water bomber.

The cockpit of a Canadair water bomber is comfortably fitted with two ergonomically designed leather seats, easy-to-read digital controls and a throttle console dividing pilot and copilot. There is plenty of visibility from the wraparound windows, and flying her empty is a joy, according to most pilots.

The FN Maximi has a rate of fire of eight hundred NATO 7.62 ammunition per minute, and Holliday kept up a continuous earsplitting barrage into the hull, cutting easily through the thin aluminum skin of the fuselage and filling the cockpit with a white-hot enraged swarm of metal wasps while Eddie's shells from the automatic rifle tore into the portside Pratt & Whitney turboprop.

The pilot, Andy Benson, his copilot, Randy Menzer, and the navigator, Jimmy Salazar, were turned into human steak tartare, Salazar with just enough time to push the pilot's remains out of the way and haul up on the yoke as another swarm of the same wasps ripped up through the floor and stole away what little remained of Jimmy's life.

Guns still blazing, the portside engine and propellers disintegrating in a comet's tail of white-hot aluminum and flames, the water bomber passed over Holliday and Eddie less than fifteen feet over their heads, barely giving them time to read the large letters spelling out FIREBREAKERS in white lettering on the underside of each wing.

'Firebreakers, my ass,' said Holliday as he and Eddie turned to watch the death of the burning aircraft. The nose seemed to rise slightly as though the plane itself were fighting for its life, but then the portside fuel tank and the engine exploded. A wing blew off and spun into the jungle, and the plane turned on its side just as it smashed into the water and went under almost instantly about a hundred yards astern of the riverboat. There was a brief moment of silence and then a huge gout of oily, smoky flame rose out of the water like hell rising from the underworld.

'Napalm,' said Holliday. The last time he'd seen it used was at Tora Bora in Afghanistan. 'That was no water bomber – it was a firebomber. And the question is, how did they know exactly where we were?'

'The people of this Firebreaker company will soon be missing their aircraft,' said Eddie, watching the flames carried downstream like a puddle of churning volcanic lava.

'Yeah, and I've got a pretty good idea about who they really are.'

Captain Ron Taylor stood above the bank of radar screens in the underground control bunker at what had once been Luke Auxiliary Air Force Base Number 11, not far from the town of Buckeye, Arizona. It was now owned by Aviation Consultation Enterprises, which owned its own air cargo company,

Redwood Air, both of which were owned in turn by White Star Protective Solutions, itself a small part of the Pallas Group. The binders needed to trace ownership of Firebreakers to A.C.E., Redwood, White Star and the Pallas Group would have been twice as thick as the Manhattan phone book.

Taylor turned to the young corporal beside him. 'Well?'

'The base in Bolívar hasn't heard from Red Two for an hour, sir.'

'Could she still be in the air?'

'Unlikely.'

'What else do we have down there?'

'Two Super Tucanos in Colombian livery, supposedly being used for aerial reconnaissance but they're completely weaponized, sir.'

'Send them both out. My orders are to kill the son of a bitch, and I intend to do just that.'

'Right away, sir.'

'And somebody get me Virginia. The boss is going to want to hear about this.'

9

Holliday and Eddie pulled a stunned Rafi from the chewed-up, splintered wreck of the wheelhouse, and then they began a frantic search for survivors. Thankfully Peggy was unharmed, having been in the big old claw-foot bathtub in their cabin trying to cool off when the bullets began to fly, and having stayed put for the duration.

The majority of the porters who set up housekeeping on the main deck between the side rails and the superstructure of the riverboat hadn't been so lucky. Most of them had been cooking their breakfasts on tiny portable stoves when the attack began, and more than a dozen had been killed outright and just as many wounded.

The SS *Amador* hadn't fared much better. Rafi had managed to run her aground on a mud bar close to the right bank, but as the seconds passed the current swung the stern of the ship downstream, giving the machine guns on the water bomber the chance for a raking broadside that ripped through the sternwheeler and the hull, destroying both boilers and mangling the steering mechanism. It was repairable, but it would require days of labor.

'This isn't going to work,' said Holliday, climbing up the metal companionway from the engine room to the deck.

'Why not, *compadre*?' Eddie asked. 'We have the tools and I have the experience. It would simply take a few days' work.'

'That's time we don't have,' said Holliday. 'They must have planted a transponder on the boat when we picked her up in São João Joaquin. It's probably still here, and they'll be coming back as soon as they figure out their Firebreaker flying boat isn't. We've got to get everything and everybody off the ship, pronto, before they get here.'

Of the nine twenty-foot Zodiac Pros and their two-hundred-and-fifty-horsepower outboards, only four were undamaged. The porters who'd survived the attack quit on the spot, and two of the Zodiacs were given to them to take the wounded back to São João.

In return for the boats, Eddie insisted the healthy porters transfer as much of the supplies as they could to the remaining Zodiacs. If Sinclair's people were behind this, they'd most likely be using Super Tucanos. If so they had two hours, three at the most, to get the hell away from the riverboat before one or more of the waspish little fighter planes arrived to do their damnedest to blow them all to hell.

'We head upstream slowly,' said Holliday as they prepared to climb into the Zodiacs. 'The planes will be looking for us, so we'll keep close to the bank of the river. If we move too fast we'll leave a muddy wake a blind man could follow. We hear the planes, we get ourselves into the undergrowth that hangs over the water and hope like hell they don't see us.'

They had barely moved three hundred yards upstream from the wreck of the sternwheeler when they again heard the drone of approaching aircraft. Holliday guided the first Zodiac into the overhanging jungle of the starboard bank, and Eddie, piloting the second inflatable, was right behind him.

Holliday prayed they were both well enough hidden and far enough away from the riverboat. He looked over his shoulder; there was a faint muddy turbulence from the prop wash of the Evinrude, but it would be hard to see from the air.

As Holliday had suspected, the planes were Super Tucanos like the ones Blackhawk Security had used in Cuba. These two were dressed up in Colombian Air Force livery with sharks' mouths painted on to the nose and the blue, gold and red roundels of the Colombian flag.

They flew in a simple one-forward, one-back-and-above formation, and they came in low. As the first plane tilted its nose slightly, it released a pair of Shrike missiles from the hard points beneath its wings, both of which howled off toward the already ravaged river-boat.

The first Tucano peeled up and away to the right while the second came in firing its wing cannons and machine guns. The second Tucano barely had time to peel left before the Shrikes hit their target and a fire-ball roared up from the wreck, obliterating what was left of the ship. The two aircraft droned off into the distance.

'Can we make it in the Zodiacs?' Peggy asked as the aircraft disappeared.

'According to Fawcett's journals, they were about a hundred and eighty miles upriver from here before they headed into the jungle. I don't want to travel at night, so that means at least three days.'

'How will we know where to get off the river?'

'The notebooks mention steep cliffs and rapids. On his diagram he called them the Falls of Babylon; there were tiers of rocks beside the rapids with cascades of foliage and giant red hibiscus flowers.'

'Let's hope they're still blooming,' said Peggy.

'And let's hope we get there first,' answered Holliday.

Dimitri Rogov, Steven Cornwell, so-called project manager of the Excalibur Marine Exploration Corporation, and Tashkin Akurgal, head of Excalibur's security division, sat around the table in the suite at the Hotel Quinto in Barcelos and stared down at the large topographical map of the Rio Negro area.

Cornwell was ex–Special Boat Squadron, his gray hair in a military cut, his hard square face tanned and seamed by a life spent in climates other than that of his native England. Akurgal was in his fifties and built like a wrestler, which he'd been in his youth, with a shaved head, dark eyebrows, a thick salt-and-pepper mustache and a long wormlike scar along his right cheek from temple to chin that he never talked about.

'Lord Grayle sent this by courier. It arrived today; it's a blowup of a map that was found in one of Fawcett's notebooks,' said Rogov.

'How the hell did he get them?' Cornwell asked. 'I thought you said the Blackstock woman wouldn't sell them.'

'She didn't know what she had at that point.' Rogov smiled. 'Then she showed them to Holliday and that was that, but when they took them to London to put them in a safe-deposit box, they got a copy of all of them made at the Colour Company on Curzon Street. Grayle had a tail on them and he bribed one of the employees to make copies. Simple.'

'Maybe it was simple to get, but what the hell does it mean?' Cornwell said, staring down at the map. It clearly showed the Xingu and Negro rivers and the land beyond it but very little more except a superimposed diagram of a dotted line with a letter at each end and beneath that a phrase. Beneath the phrase was a symbol:

$$N \ldots\ldots\ldots\ldots\ldots\ldots\ldots\ldots\ldots R$$

by the Compass and the Square

Rogov explained, 'According to Grayle, the phrase is a coded Masonic greeting, among other things. The compass and the square are two of the three "Great Lights." The third Great Light was originally the Ark of the Covenant but is now generally thought to be the Old Testament.'

'And the line with the two letters?'

'Grayle has a theory about that. His grandfather backed Fawcett's last expedition, but in the end Fawcett never returned. The symbol was a clue meant for a fellow Mason, which both Fawcett and Grayle's grandfather were. The compass forms two sides of an equilateral triangle, the base of which is the line with the two letters. Fawcett's Lost City was the third point of the triangle – the hinge on the compass.'

'But what good does that do us?' Cornwell asked. 'You have to know what the two letters stand for and how long the line really is in geographical terms.'

'And that's the problem we have to solve before Holliday does. We must first of all get ahead of him. The transponder is still operating. He's heading in a northerly direction. According to the notebooks, Fawcett entered the jungle at a place he called the Falls of Babylon, a large set of rapids and cliffs . . . here.' He pointed to a written notation on the enlarged copy of the map. 'We get there first and ambush them.'

'We kill them, yes?' Akurgal the Turk asked, a glint in his eye.

'First we talk. Then we kill,' said Rogov.

10

On their first night in the inflatables, they drew the two Zodiacs into a small, vine-enclosed backwater on the right bank that would be invisible both from the water and the air. The water in the little inlet was black as ink and covered with some kind of water lily. Directly above them vines and moss hung down in great sweeping curves, and above that was the distant rainforest canopy itself. The air was breath-snatchingly hot and their clothes were damp with sweat. The inlet smelled heavily of rotting vegetation, and all around and above them was the chattering, clicking and screeching of creatures hiding in the shadows of the dying day.

They had pulled the two Zodiacs together for the night. Tanaki had used his fragile little bow and arrow to capture a pair of zebra catfish, and his grandfather Nenderu was cooking some sort of stew he'd made of the fish and local vegetation, boiling it all in a collapsible leather pot over the low flame of the expedition's Primus stove.

'My grandfather says he likes your fire in a bottle very much,' said Tanaki.

'Tell him he can have it if we get out of this alive,' answered Holliday, flipping through the notebooks, looking for some clue as to where to go next.

'A lot of bugs and things in places like this?' Peggy asked Tanaki.

'Tarantulas, wolf spiders, poisonous caterpillars, several kinds of scorpions. The jungle is not a very inviting place, missy. There are also caimans, like alligators, boas, anacondas, bushmasters . . . fire ants.'

'Which is why we sleep under these,' said Holliday as he and Eddie began to slide together the poles that made up the twin mosquito nets that enclosed the Zodiacs.

'You sure would make a hell of a salesman for Amazon Tours,' said Peggy to Tanaki. 'Come to a land of enchantment where caimans eat you by day and giant anacondas swallow you whole.'

'Don't forget the bushmasters,' added Rafi, dishing out Nenderu's fragrant stew.

With the mosquito nets to protect them, the group settled in for the night.

'We're supposed to sleep through all that?' Peggy asked, staring up through the netting. The sound was deafening, worse than it was during the day. Insects, night birds, larger creatures coughing, barking or growling. Peggy had always thought of the rainforest in almost a spiritual way: the grandeur of the canopy, the rainforest as the living, breathing lungs of the earth. She'd just never expected the lungs to be quite so noisy and quite so . . . real. Animals ate other animals, scorpions stung spiders, snakes killed monkeys – things died here all the time and they rotted, and what didn't rot, the bugs ate.

'Just what the hell are we doing here?' Peggy asked. A giant brown moth landed on the netting six inches from her face, and she screamed. 'Son of a bitch!'

'It's a giant silk moth,' answered Rafi, 'nothing to be frightened about, sweetie.'

'Don't you sweetie me! This place is a horror show. Nobody in their right mind would come here!'

'Peggy's got a point, you know,' said Holliday thoughtfully, leaning back on the heavy rubber inflatable hull.

'Peggy's always got a point,' said Rafi, grinning fondly at his wife and squeezing her hand.

'I'm being serious,' said Holliday. 'Fawcett looked for his lost city everywhere but north. On his last expedition, financed by latter-day Templars, he comes up the Xingu River – clearly with the first Lord Grayle and his White Gloves pulling the strings.'

'Wasn't that because of the ships Fawcett discovered?' Peggy asked, snuggling into her husband's enfolding arm.

'That's what I thought originally, but now I'm not so sure.'

'Why?' Rafi asked.

'The First Lord Grayle was a businessman, a banker, in fact. I can see how a man of that period could get caught up in Fawcett's dreams of lost worlds and limitless gold. Fawcett was even friends with Arthur Conan Doyle, the man who wrote *The Lost World*. That kind of thing holds a fascination for nearly everyone.' Holliday paused. 'On the other hand the present Lord Grayle is the largest privatizer of water resources in the world among other things. I doubt that he's got a romantic bone in his body.'

'You're saying this all has to do with water?' Rafi asked.

'Not necessarily,' said Holliday. 'But think about it. Rogov's one of Grayle's men and he's been on us from the start. We're following in Fawcett's footsteps to some unknown destination that might give us some answers, but Grayle knows exactly what he's after. You don't firebomb people just for the fun of it. And don't forget those fighter planes. I guarantee you they came from whatever Kate Sinclair calls her private army of thugs these days. This whole thing is big and we don't even really know what it is.'

Dimitri Rogov, Steven Cornwell and Tashkin Akurgal flew the ancient single-engine de Havilland Beaver low over the jungle, moving steadily north, keeping the winding path of the Xingu far to the left; the last thing Rogov wanted to do was alert Holliday that they were getting ahead of them.

'You think maybe you could have found a better plane than this old crate?' Cornwell said, squirming on the cracked vinyl seat. 'It's got to be fifty years old.'

'More like sixty,' answered Rogov. 'In the middle of Brazil, beggars can't be choosers. You've been living in the lap of your master's luxury for far too long, *muy droog.*'

'Your master, as well, Rogov, and don't you forget it.'

The Russian turned in the pilot's seat, his face gone suddenly dark. As if by magic a little Beretta Bobcat appeared in his hand, the pocket semi-automatic a few inches from the Englishman's face. 'Know this, my Anglo friend. No man is my master, not even your Lord Grayle. He has set me a task and I will do it and then I shall go my own way once more. Tell me you understand this, or my little gun will blow your brains through the window behind you and then your corpse will follow for the beetles and the flies to feed on.'

For a moment Cornwell returned Rogov's malevolent stare with his own, but eventually he nodded.

'Good,' said the Russian, and they flew on.

Rogov recognized Fawcett's Gardens of Babylon immediately: great slabs of dark rock in geometric tiers rising at least two hundred feet into the air, the broader slabs interspersed with narrower ones that jutted out slightly, each one covered in frothy cascades of gigantic pink and purple and yellow blooms, long tendrils of leaf-covered vine and drooping beards of heavy-hanging moss.

In the center was the waterfall itself, a great curtain of water streaming down in a rainbow torrent that struck the river below, throwing up the gentle mist that made the blooms glisten in the late afternoon sun. It was a magnificent sight, and Rogov couldn't have cared less for the great natural beauty beneath his wings. The only thing that pleased him was the fact that there was no sign of John Holliday.

He took the old single-engine plane a little more than half a mile upriver from the falls and then landed. He let the de Havilland drift down on the current, using the pontoon rudders to keep the plane close to shore.

Eventually he spotted the place he wanted and switched on the engine again, forcing the aircraft up on to the muddy foreshore until the portside pontoon was hard aground.

'Why this filthy spot?' grunted Cornwell, staring out of the plane's window at the mud.

'Because we're going to need this little bird when we come back this way and I want her to be here when we do,' said Rogov. 'We'll tie the old bird up, get out our goods and then find a place to hit Holliday and his friends.'

Francisco Garibaldi, playing the part of Lord Jonathon Gibbs, third Baron Vauxhall, sat in the dining hall of Stonehurst Hall perfectly dressed in evening clothes, as were the other guests around the table, most of whom had come for the grouse shooting the following day. The women were equally well dressed, including Grayle's dark-haired and extremely aristocratic-looking wife, the Duchess Caroline, who, by Garibaldi's estimation, appeared to be at the top of the social heap among the women, all of whom were the wives of earls, viscounts, marquises and a few barons and baronets at the bottom of the heap. The priest was glad he'd studied up on terms of address on the plane in from Rome; one misstep and he would have been exposed as the imposter he was.

The meal, served by assorted footmen, with Beamish, Lord Grayle's butler, pouring the wine, was a little extreme for Garibaldi's slightly more plebeian taste: oysters, watercress soup, shrimp mousse, filet mignon, rack of lamb or roast squab, all with asparagus vinaigrette and pâté de foie gras, followed by a fruit and cheese plate and a variety of pastries. Each course was served with the appropriate hock, burgundy, Chablis, sherry or port.

Eventually all good things came to an end. The

women withdrew to the drawing room, leaving the men to their brandy and their cigars. After half an hour of discussion, mostly about the relative qualities and differences between Purdey Doubles and Holland & Holland Over-and-Unders, the men 'went through' and joined the women. Grayle hung back.

'A word?' Grayle said to Garibaldi.

'Certainly, Your Grace,' the priest replied.

'In the library, then,' said Grayle, ushering Garibaldi through a pair of ornate doors and into a large room. The walls were covered with books that looked as old as some of the ones in the Vatican Library. The high, ornate ceiling featured a central frieze that seemed to depict the Battle of Waterloo in excruciating detail.

'Whiskey?' Grayle asked, half filling a crystal tumbler at a drink stand off to one side.

'No, thank you,' said Garibaldi.

'Do sit,' said the duke, indicating a comfortable club chair. The priest did so and Grayle followed suit, sitting across from him. 'Now, then,' said Grayle, taking a swallow from his glass. 'Let's get down to business, shall we?'

'Certainly,' said Garibaldi.

'The last time we met, you said you had something you wanted to show me. What is it?'

Garibaldi reached into the pocket of his dinner jacket and took out a single large, uncut and unpolished diamond. He leaned forward and placed it on the burled walnut table between them. Grayle picked up the stone and hefted it in his hand.

'Twenty carats in the rough,' he said. 'And it's not alluvial. It's from a kimberlite pipe.'

'That's right,' said Garibaldi.

'South Africa?'

'No, Your Grace. Brazil.'

'I don't believe you. There are no pipes large enough to mine this size in Brazil.'

'Yes, there are,' said Garibaldi. 'This diamond was mined there four hundred years ago.'

I I

Holliday and the others arrived at the Gardens of Babylon in the late afternoon of the following day. They found the small cove and the broad brown sand beach exactly the way Fawcett had described it in his secret journal. Above the beach was a large shelf of slatelike stone. In the journals, Fawcett wrote that he had decided to camp there. Beyond the shelf of rock, the jungle began.

'If it was good enough for old Percy,' said Peggy, 'I guess it's good enough for us.'

They pulled the Zodiacs as far up the beach as possible, then drove pegs deep into the sand and tied the boats down. They threw out the claw anchors for each craft, then ran lines from the boats up on to the rocks, where they drove pitons between the layers of rock, further securing the inflatables.

'What's with the sudden interest in keeping the boats secure?' Peggy asked.

'Because the water level is fickle,' Holliday answered. 'It can rise four or five feet in a few weeks. We're just making sure they're here when we get back. Who knows how long this whole thing is going to take?'

'Days, weeks, maybe even longer,' said Rafi. 'For some reason Fawcett didn't date his entries, so it makes it tough to figure out a timeline.' He added, 'My stomach says it's time to eat something.'

The old man Nenderu gathered wood from the edge of the forest and made a fire while Tanaki disappeared into the jungle carrying his blowpipe, his bow, a quiver of arrows at his hip and his long steel-tipped spear.

He was back twenty minutes later with a ten-pound spider monkey slung over his shoulder. Peggy watched in horror as he gutted, skinned and butchered the carcass down into its basic parts. He took the meat, including the heart, to Nenderu, who skewered the pieces on a makeshift spit over the coals of the fire.

He paid special attention to the head, which he wrapped in broad banana leaves and stuffed deeply into the glowing coals, almost covering the dark green package.

Meanwhile Tanaki took several banana leaves and bound them together into a large, boatlike vessel. He piled the offal from the monkey into the interior of the banana leaves and then handed it to his grandfather. Nenderu took it to the edge of the river and squatted down beside the water and began to sing loftily in a lilting, eerie undertone.

'What is he doing?' Peggy asked Tanaki.

'He is making an offering to the river and to the jungle.'

Nenderu pushed the raft of banana leaves and offal into the water, where it quickly drifted into the main current. Fifty feet downstream from the camp, there was a sudden flurry in the water and a pair of snapping reptilian jaws swallowed the offering whole.

'What the hell was that!' Peggy yelped.

'Caiman. Like an alligator,' said Tanaki.

'They're in the river?'

'And on the land. They lay their eggs by the edge of the water. Sometimes they come on land to hunt,' replied the Indian.

'Relax, Peg, you can always hear them coming.' Holliday smiled.

'How's that?' Peggy asked suspiciously.

'You can hear the alarm clock ticking in his stomach,' laughed Rafi.

'Ha-ha,' said Peggy.

Half an hour later the meat was ready and Nenderu served it out on the aluminum plates they all carried in their packs. The meat was surprisingly tender and perfectly cooked. According to Tanaki, this was because the monkeys ate almost nothing but fruits and nuts.

As the meal ended, there was a distinct popping noise from the center of the coals. Nenderu dug out his banana-leaf-wrapped package and set it down on the rock. He unwrapped the banana leaves and withdrew the steaming head of the monkey.

The popping sound had been caused by the bursting of the skull. Borrowing Tanaki's broad-bladed hunting knife, Nenderu pried the skull fully open, revealing the parboiled brain of the creature. He reached into the opening and, using three fingers, spooned out a large lump of the gray-white stuff and handed it around. Eddie took it enthusiastically.

'We have something like this in Cuba,' he said. '*Buñuelos de seso.*'

'Brain fritters,' said Holliday. 'I'll try some of that.'

'I think I'm going to be sick,' groaned Peggy, turning her face away from the sight of the steaming monkey brain.

With dinner finally over, Eddie and Holliday cleaned up while Peggy and Rafi got out the sleeping gear and began to set up the tents and the mosquito netting for the night ahead.

With the tents up and darkness falling quickly over the jungle, Holliday noticed that Tanaki was crouched by the water's edge, dragging his fingers through the water. Holliday joined him, squatting down beside the Indian. From his expression, there was no doubt something was bothering him.

'What's the matter?' Holliday asked.

Tanaki lifted his fingers out of the water and rubbed them together. 'Oil,' he said.

'Could it be from the Zodiacs?'

'Look,' said Tanaki. In the last of the fading light, Holliday could see a shimmering iridescent slick that began well ahead of their landing spot. 'It comes from above the high water,' said Tanaki.

'An outboard from some little village upstream?'

'The only villages upstream belong to the Kayapo, who have no boats with engines, and anyway, the oil is much too heavy.'

'An airplane?' asked Holliday.

'I think so, and not too far from here or the oil would have been carried to the middle of the stream and would not be so visible.'

'We've got trouble, then.'

'Bad trouble.' Tanaki nodded. 'Very bad.'

Lord Grayle had offered Francisco Garibaldi the use of his personal GJ, but the killer priest much preferred commercial flight for the sake of anonymity. The Virgin Atlantic flight from Heathrow to Georgetown, Guyana, was twenty-odd hours long, including a two-hour layover in Boston that gave him plenty of time to recall the details of his conversation with Grayle and to plan out his modus operandi. The story he told to His Lordship was complicated and long, and his response had been predictable.

'According to the detailed Templar records kept in the Vatican Secret Archives, in April 1437 three ships left the Port of Lisbon. They were the *Santo Antonio de Padua*, the *Santo Ovidio de Braga* and the *Santo João de Deus*. According to your company, Excalibur Marine Exploration, the *Santo Antonio de Padua* contained twelve tons of gold Charles the Fifth francs. Supposedly they were to be delivered to a secret hiding place somewhere in South America.

'Also according to your company, the *Santo Antonio de Padua* and the other two ships became separated during a hurricane of immense force, probably a category five, much worse than Hurricane Katrina.

'Most of what your company reported was untrue, either because you were trying to lift the stock price of Excalibur or more likely you didn't want the public to know what the *Santo Antonio de Padua* really contained, which was absolutely nothing, a fact you knew from the beginning.'

'Perhaps you can explain,' Lord Grayle responded when the priest had finished speaking, 'why an empty ship was found that was supposed to be delivering a hoard of gold to a secret hiding place somewhere up the Amazon.'

'The answer is simple,' said Garibaldi. 'The *Santo Antonio de Padua* was empty because she wasn't *approaching* the mouth of the Amazon. She was leaving it, her great and most holy accomplishment already completed.'

'And what holy accomplishment would that be?' Grayle asked.

Garibaldi paused before he spoke. 'The delivery of the holy relics from the hidden chambers far beneath the Bet HaMikdash, the Holy Temple on Temple Mount in Jerusalem.'

'And what holy relics would those have been?' Grayle's skepticism seemed to be growing with every sentence.

'The Ark of the Covenant and all that it contained – the broken pieces of the tablets Moses brought down from Mount Sinai, the copy that was made from them, the iron head of the spear that pierced Christ's side, sometimes referred to as the Spear of Destiny, the spiked iron crown of thorns placed around His head as a further torture, the eight nails used to crucify Him, the shroud He was wrapped in and the ossuary that holds the remains of His earthly body left behind – His bones.'

'Absurd,' Grayle said. 'Everything you mentioned is nothing more than a myth that has gained complexity over time.'

'You are certainly right when you say the stories of the relics have been made elaborately complex over time, but think carefully. Crucifixion was a common form of punishment during the time of Christ, and using spikes to fix Him to the cross was a particularly vile form of the punishment.

'The legionaries of the Fourth Thracum Syriaca who occupied Jerusalem at the time of Christ's death were an auxiliary legion and known for being particularly cruel and undisciplined, hence the crown of thorns and the spear.

'After the death of Christ, His family and His disciples would have gathered up the body, the spearhead, the nails and the crown of thorns and taken everything away for proper burial, which would account for the shroud. Fearing, quite correctly, that Christ's earthly body would not be resurrected, they removed it from the tomb and took the body elsewhere, also concluding that those same legionaries who had defiled Him on the cross would defile and ridicule His corpse in its tomb.

'A year or two later they collected the bones and placed them in a chalk ossuary or burial box sixteen inches high and thirty-one inches long. These were all later placed in the Ark of the Covenant, which was described as being a wooden box four and a quarter feet long, two and a half feet high and two and a half feet wide.

'There are a great many stories about it being covered in gold with winged cherubim on the lid, but once again those are all hypothetical since the Ark was covered in a leather and wool *parokta*, or veil, at all times, and not even the priests were allowed to see it. At any rate, it was more than large enough to carry all the relics from Christ's Crucifixion and later burial.'

'And you're saying the Ark and all these relics within it were taken to the Amazon aboard the *Santo Antonio de Padua*? For what possible reason?' Grayle asked, laughing. 'The whole thing's just a load of tosh.'

Garibaldi continued his story. 'The relics were taken by a group of dedicated and battle-hardened Templar warriors to the last secret stronghold of the Templar order deep in the jungles of northern Amazonia. The same place your grandfather and his White Gloves paid Percy Fawcett to find.' Garibaldi paused. 'The same place these came from.'

He reached into the other pocket of his evening jacket and brought out a black velvet drawstring bag. He tipped the contents out on to the parquetry table beside Lord Grayle's chair. A heap of diamonds cascaded out, some even larger than the single twenty-carat stone he'd shown Grayle before. 'A kimberlite pipe so rich it has more stones than all of South Africa has mined in the last one hundred years. With this mine in your hands, you could corner the market in industrial- and gem-quality diamonds for the rest of time.'

'And if I was to believe this twaddle you've been handing me,' Grayle replied, 'why on earth would I believe that you'd simply hand this enormously valuable asset to me on a platter, so to speak?'

'Because I'm appealing to your nature and your inclination as a businessman. You know as well as I do that the White Gloves, a latter-day version of the Templars, are just as much interested in money as the original Templars were.

'The Templars were no religious order, Lord Grayle. They were a power-accumulating and power-mongering bunch of thieves, murderers and blackmailers who used the Holy Mother Church and the Crusades as a rationale for plundering their way across the Middle East and back again. There's really very little difference in our purposes here; the Vatican is as much in business as we are.'

'A business that's been taking some bad hits on the public relations side of things. Child abuse, pedophiles, homosexuals and the like, I might add.'

'I assure you, Lord Grayle, we are quite aware of our own shortcomings, but like any business or any other organization, there are going to be bad apples. I'm also willing to lay odds that there are proportionately just as many so-called deviants among your own members of parliament and the House of Lords, or in the American House or Senate. People in glass houses really shouldn't be throwing stones; there's no telling what you might find underneath those particular rocks.'

'Touché, but why don't we get down to brass tacks? What exactly do you want from me?'

'We need those relics; their discovery would go a long way toward bolstering the Church's reputation.'

'What exactly do I get in return?'

'You tell me everything you know about Holliday's expedition. I give you access to the diamonds, you give the relics to the Church and we both get Colonel John Holliday dead.'

Arriving in Georgetown after midnight, Father Francisco Garibaldi, traveling on his own passport once again, booked himself into a pleasant room at the Pegasus Hotel and got a good night's sleep. Following breakfast he had a quick tour of the old Dutch Colonial city before heading to the airport and boarding an Air Guyana Cessna Caravan for the short trip to the town of Bartica at the mouth of the Essequibo River.

Dimitri Rogov, Steven Cornwell and Tashkin Akurgal waited above the trail in a blind Akurgal had built using mosquito netting, leaves and branches from the surrounding jungle. Beside them a thin stream trickled down from some unseen place above them, crossing the trail a hundred yards farther down the slope.

'Why don't they move?' Cornwell said, irritated. The pinger on the GPS unit that lay at their feet kept giving out a steady, strong and unmoving signal. Somewhere on the long journey to this place in the jungle, Grayle's people had managed to plant a GPS transponder in the thick nylon heel of Holliday's sturdy, brand-new combat boot and into the tubing of the pack frame he used. If Holliday went anywhere on the planet, Rogov's GPS unit would know it.

'We cannot wait here forever,' muttered Akurgal the Turk. He squeezed the head off a six- or seven-inch centipede, avoiding its flailing, long-pincered tail. 'Stay much longer and we'll be eaten alive.'

'If Holliday is going to follow in the footsteps of this Percy, he is going to have to get off his ass sometime.'

'Bloody hell!' Cornwell bellowed, slapping at his cheek. The bellow became a screech of agony. 'Get it off! Get it off!'

'It is off,' said the Turk. He took out one of the foul-smelling cigars he favored, lit it with an old Ronson and puffed.

Rogov stared at Cornwell's cheek: there was a bright red spot in the middle and a stream of puslike venom dripping out of the center.

The Turk leaned over casually and jammed the hot end of the cigar on to the spot, grinding it in. Cornwell's screech turned into a bloodcurdling scream and he jerked away from the burning cigar tip. 'What are you fucking doing!' Cornwell moaned.

'You struck an assassin bug. The bug struck back,' explained the Turk. 'The longer the venom stays beneath your skin, the more it spreads. Some people who are allergic can die from the bite of such a creature. The only way to stop it from spreading is by burning it out. You should thank me, Englishman. I did you good favor.'

'What is that smell?' Rogov said, an urgent tone in his voice.

'My bloody roasting flesh!' Cornwell snarled, holding his neckerchief over the wound on his face.

'Not that smell, you idiot!' Rogov put his nose into the air. 'That smell!'

The Turk sniffed loudly. Then his eyes widened with fear. 'Fire!'

Holliday, never the most trusting of old friends, was particularly leery about friends who were still active mercenaries like Chang-Su Diaz, the ex-Ranger pilot who'd bought their supplies and flown them upriver to São João Joaquin. Holliday and Eddie had spent a lot of time on their upriver trek to the Gardens of Babylon going over the equipment with a fine-tooth comb.

Eddie found the first bug, buried in the pack frame, and after that it hadn't been too difficult to find the one in the Magnum combat boot – the scratches around the heel had been a dead giveaway. Instead of destroying them, Holliday slipped them carefully into the pocket of his jacket. Knowing someone was trying to follow you was one thing; being able to fool them about your location was even better.

He assumed it was either Rogov or Grayle on his trail; not that it mattered – they were on the same team.

Early that morning Eddie and Holliday had scouted the way ahead looking for likely ambush positions, and it hadn't taken them more than an hour or so to find the deep cut with the little stream running through it.

'This is it,' said Holliday.

Eddie nodded. 'It is perfect,' he agreed. The tall Cuban slipped off the trail and up into the jungle. Holliday waited. Eddie reappeared a few minutes later.

'We were right, amigo. Twenty yards down the trail and above it, they have a . . . In Spanish it is an *escondite de caza.*'

'A hunting blind,' offered Holliday.

'*Sí*, and a blind man must have built it. The thing is very ugly.'

'Empty?'

'For now.' Eddie nodded.

From fifty feet above the hunting blind, Eddie watched as the fire he'd started with a can of outboard fuel and an emergency flare roared down on Rogov and his men. Eddie had the gas can in one hand, and on the unlikely chance that one of the men came uphill through the fire, he had one of the Stoner light machine guns in the other.

He could already hear them panicking in the blind as the thick gray smoke began to roll over them while the fire burned through the damp rain forest underbrush.

Below, on the trail, Holliday waited, kneeling on one leg, the futuristic Heckler & Koch MSG-90 sniper rifle balanced across his thigh. The smoke was getting thicker as it oozed down the hillside, and Holliday could hear the crackling of the flames.

He lifted the lightweight rifle to his shoulder and flicked off the safety, then thumbed the selector to single-shot fire. The flames were roaring now. He aimed, gauging roughly where their adversaries would appear. The rifle had a twenty-round box magazine and according to Eddie, the blind on the high ground was only large enough for four or five at the most.

Holliday watched the fire's progress; he could see an orange glow from the dense smoke less than fifty feet above the trail; it wouldn't be long now. A billow of smoke wafted across the clearing, and Holliday tensed. Suddenly a crouching shadow appeared, a moving, scuttling object almost invisible in the screening fog.

Holliday squeezed the trigger, aiming for what he hoped was center mass. A crack of sound reverberated from the rifle, but the crouching figure made it to the other side of the trail and vanished.

A second figure appeared, stumbling and coughing in the haze. This target was much larger than the one before – Holliday fired a second time and there was a scream, but it was the sound of a man barely hit, perhaps no more than a graze. The third man was obviously confused; Holliday could see his arms flailing in the smoke. Holliday took his time. The first shot hit high, throwing the man into a spin that took him halfway to the other side of the trail.

Holliday adjusted his aim and fired again and the man dropped. There was a flurry of movement as the wounded man was dragged away and a rattle of gunfire sounded from an automatic weapon. Holliday recognized the tooth-chattering drumroll of an AK-47 on full auto and dropped to the right, knee-and elbowing his way backward down the trail, so close to the ground he could almost taste the rot-richness of the thick black soil. He found a tree and rolled behind it. There was a pause as the shooter changed clips and then another spray of fire howled along the trail. Then there was silence.

13

'So, what is your plan?' Akurgal said, staring down at the groaning man lying on the ground in the middle of their camp. Wisps of smoke trailed all around them, some of it drifting down around the floats of the beached airplane and out over the river. 'Unless he gets to a hospital, he is going to die.' Akurgal ignored the blood dripping from his own torn ear where the bullet had clipped him, but there was no ignoring the wounds to Cornwell's shoulder and right side. There was blood everywhere, and the blood on the Englishman's side was dark and arterial – probably from his liver.

'Dear Christ, get me out of here,' whispered Cornwell, his eyes pleading, his breath coming in short, sharp gasps.

'Come with me,' said Rogov to Akurgal. The two men walked down to the beach and looked back up toward the trail. He kept his voice low. 'If we take him back to Bartica, not only will we have to answer awkward questions about how he was shot, but we will lose Holliday and any chance of finding Fawcett's treasure.'

'He will die if we leave him here,' Akurgal said.

'He might die anyway,' said Rogov. 'We cannot wait on this forever.'

'No,' said Akurgal. 'This is true.'

'Then we are agreed?'

'Yes.'

They went back up to Cornwell. The bleeding was even worse now, but he was still conscious.

'What are you doing?' Cornwell groaned as the huge Turk gathered the much smaller man into his arms. He took him thirty feet or so down to the edge of the river while Rogov, following, rummaged around in his pack.

'Taking you to the hospital, of course,' answered Akurgal. 'Mr Rogov has to prepare the aircraft for you.' He laid the injured Englishman down in the mud and stood back.

Rogov screwed the TROS Diplomat-II suppressor to the HK P9S from his pack and shot Cornwell twice in the face. His nose and mouth disintegrated, and the back of his head blew out into the mud. Together Rogov and Akurgal dragged the body into the water and pushed it into the current.

Cardinal secretary of state Arturo Bonnifacio Ruffino sat at the long table in the conference room of the euphemistically and somewhat evasively named Institute for the Works of Religion – popularly and more accurately known as the Vatican Bank – and stared up at the ceiling. It wasn't quite a typical ceiling for a bank; in fact, most shareholders in an ordinary bank would have tossed out the CEO for wasting so much money on a space with such a poor location. The Vatican was housed in the Apostolic Palace in a building that once served as a jail for heretics and other nonsecular prisoners. Fast-forward several hundred years, and the ceiling of what was now used as a conference room was a good runner-up to the Sistine Chapel for exuberant decoration.

A single gigantic allegorical painting stretched across the ceiling, showing the Virgin Mary somewhat improbably wearing a papal tiara and holding a model of a church. Another holy lady offered the mother of Jesus a gold plate laden with crowns, a gold chain and an honorific decoration. In the background, Neptune emerged from the sea on a chariot, while in the foreground a snake wound its way through a patch of mushrooms.

The cardinal could figure most of it out, all except the mushrooms. The only time mushrooms appeared in the Bible was in Exodus when manna from heaven was being described, but a snake in the manna? It didn't seem like much of an allegory.

The marble table was almost as ornate as the ceiling – intertwining vines and snakes, women carrying vases and floral motifs. It was twenty feet long, seven feet wide and was actually a leftover slab of flooring from Siena Cathedral. Around the table were thirteen men, including the president of the Vatican Bank, the vice president and the chief financial officer, as well as accountants and members of the cardinal's oversight committee. There was a fourteenth chair at the far end of the table reserved out of respect for the Holy Father, but as far as anyone knew he'd never occupied it.

'So, Cardinal Ruffino, how goes it with the negotiations with Lord Grayle and his White Horse Resources?' The query came from Francisco Neri, the most powerful member of the so-called Black Nobility – aristocrats with either a direct family connection to the papacy or ones owed a number of favors by the Vatican.

'Well enough, Signor Neri,' Ruffino answered. 'One must step carefully when walking with dangerous men.'

'And he is, of course, Templarii, as we all know.'

'Grayle is a man of business before he is a Templar,' said the cardinal, 'and he does not take it kindly that you have purchased every available share of his corporation you could get your hands on.'

'It has always been this bank's practice to keep its enemies close, Your Eminence. What better way to keep him close than to buy him?'

'Or to make him suspicious of our motives.'

'You sit in your office and think lofty thoughts about foreign policy, and all the while the Church is the next best thing to bankrupt. Somebody has to think of the finances of Holy Mother Church or it will cease to exist.'

'And you think an interest in White Horse Resources will give the Church that sort of relief?' asked Cardinal Ruffino.

'A holding interest would give us a foothold.'

'Grayle will never allow it.'

'Then perhaps we should try for a hostile one. We don't have the capital, but we are friends with enough banks to get it.'

'He'd strip his assets and dissolve the company before you made your first telephone call.'

Neri gave Ruffino a scornful look. 'And thus destroy an enemy. It seems worth a phone call, Your Eminence.'

'Should I really take you for such a fool, Signor Neri,' the cardinal replied, 'or your friend Archbishop Abanndando beside you?'

Abanndando was an immensely fat man with a taste for handsome young priests, or even younger altar boys, when he could get them. More than once Ruffino had thought of placing an anonymous call to the press about this pig of a man. He knew nothing of real love, only satisfying his lusts. Abanndando suffered from asthma and wheezed when he spoke.

'Your predecessor Cardinal Spada knew his place in the order of things. He always followed the advice of this institution. He did not profess to know the ins and outs of his finance, Your Eminence,' chided the fat man.

Ruffino gave him a sour look. 'He knew the ins and outs of this bank better than you know the ins and outs of an altar boy, Ab.' There was dead silence around the table. Abanndando turned the color of a ripe tomato and he began to wheeze and gasp so violently that Neri had to guide him from the room.

'There was no need for that, Your Eminence,' said Vincent Lamberto, the chairman of the bank.

'There was every reason for it, Lamberto. Settling lawsuits about creatures like Abanndando is one of the things that have put the bank in this position. From my lofty ivory tower I can sometimes see the larger picture, and this I know already – a little more than seven hundred years ago we took Grayle's forebears, and we excommunicated, imprisoned, tortured and eventually burned them at the stake, all because of money, all because a king would not pay his debts. This man and others like him have been our enemies for the better part of a millennium. A hostile takeover would only rain God knows what kind of horrors on the Church.'

Federico Mancini, the vice president of international banking, spoke up. Mancini was a force to be reckoned with despite his mild appearance and soft voice. Perhaps he was the snake in the mushrooms – the reptile at your feet you don't see until it's too late.

'So what are you suggesting?'

'Extend the hand of friendship,' said Ruffino. 'The Church needs allies now, not enemies.'

'Will Grayle take that hand?' Mancini asked.

The cardinal smiled. 'If he doesn't, then we shall cut his off.'

'We cannot stay here,' said Eddie, back at the camp by the river. 'They will ambush us one by one.'

Tanaki and his grandfather Nenderu nodded. 'And they will expect us to come up the trail again. For now it is the only way to reach our destination,' Tanaki said.

'Then, for now, we'll have to find another way,' said Holliday.

'Such as?' Peggy asked.

'We cross the river and find a way up the bluffs on the other side,' Holliday said. 'There must be some crossing farther upriver.'

'Shuar,' said Nenderu, shaking his old head. He and Tanaki spoke briefly, and then Tanaki translated for Holliday.

'My grandfather said there are bands of Shuar on the other side. Very dangerous. They are headhunters and quick to anger. They have no lands of their own and steal from others to live.'

'I thought the Shuars were only in Ecuador and Peru,' said Rafi.

'This was true, and most have been "civilized" by the white man, but some stay with the old ways, shrinking heads and eating marrow from cracked bones.'

'Wonderful.' Peggy grimaced. 'Head-shrinking cannibals.'

'If I had a choice between Rogov and the cannibals, I'd take the cannibals every time,' Holliday replied. 'Get the boats ready.'

Father Francisco Garibaldi arrived in Bartica and was pleased to see that the equipment he'd sent to Lord Grayle was ready and waiting for him, courtesy of White Horse Resources.

At the rudimentary Bartica Airstrip, he found a man named Cyril Gomes, who owned a very old Cessna 185 Skywagon floatplane and was more than happy to take him anywhere he wanted to go. Gomes was dark and mostly bald, with a salt-and-pepper mustache and a face that looked as if it were made to be a mug shot. Garibaldi, dressed in full jungle gear, handed the Guyanese man a scrap of paper with the coordinates for Holliday's last-known location.

'This place, she's in Brazil, you know?' cautioned Gomes.

'I know.'

'Going to cost you some more, man.'

'Not a problem.'

'Maybe lots more.'

'Whatever you want. Just get me there as soon as you can,' said Garibaldi.

Gomes came up with a figure and Garibaldi paid him without hesitation, using the American dollars he'd converted at the hotel that morning. He stuffed his two duffel bags and the leather gun case through the cargo hatch, then climbed into the copilot's seat while Gomes topped up the gas with a fifty-gallon drum and a hand pump.

Garibaldi noticed that despite the aircraft's age, it had a fully updated suite of avionics, including a Garmin GPS digital mapping screen, autopilot, digital weather radar and every other bell and whistle you could think of. Gomes climbed up into the pilot's seat, hit the starter and gave the engine a moment to spool up.

'You have a gun case, I saw.'

'What of it?' Garibaldi replied.

'Where you want to go is a preserve for the *indios* and the forest. Also it is illegal to bring weapons into Guyana.'

'Are you trying to get more money, Gomes? You

really think that's the smart thing to try on someone who knows how to get guns into this kaka hole of jungle you call a country? Move your stink pokie, auntie man, and move it now.'

Gomes stared at Garibaldi, utterly confused and equally afraid of this man who could suddenly speak Creole and who could look at him with such fury in his eyes. 'Ah go di it, mon, right away, sure.' Without another word the Guyanese man hauled back on the throttle, and the little one-engine plane hurtled down the dirt strip. He slipped on his headphones and mumbled something incomprehensible into the microphone. Then at sixty-five miles per hour, Gomes hauled back on the yoke and the little plane jumped almost frantically into the air. As a pilot the nasty little man certainly left a lot to be desired.

Gomes brought up the spindly landing gear into their slots on the floats, then slipped the Cessna to the west until he found the broad reaches of the Essequibo River. He turned due south before setting the Garmin GPS and the autopilot. According to the altimeter they were flying at three thousand feet, the river and the mangrove swamps on either bank of the endless snaking river nothing more than a blur.

'We go like this for an hour, boss. That way we look like we're running a tourist trip of fishermen to the tourist places. At least that's what the radar at Boa Vista going to think. Then we drop down to five hundred feet like we're landing and sneak over the border that way. Another forty minutes after that and we get you where you want to go, boss.'

'Excellent.'

They flew on in silence, Garibaldi lost in thought, preparing himself for the hunt that lay ahead. His orders from Grayle required him to find the exact location of the kimberlite pipe containing the diamonds and to assassinate Holliday and any other members of his party.

His orders from the Vatican differed only slightly; when he'd discovered the kimberlite deposit, he was also to confirm the presence of the relics, and after killing Holliday he was to assassinate Grayle and as many of the members of the White Glove Society as he thought feasible.

In his mind's eye, Garibaldi kept on seeing the fleeting image of Archbishop Gilday, robes fluttering as he was tossed off the spiral staircase in the Vatican Museums. Not as far from the truth as most people thought, and much further from the truth than he'd ever imagined when he was ordained a priest.

As Gomes promised, a little more than an hour after taking off he slipped on the headset, muttering into the microphone, then flipped off the autopilot. 'I tell them we are going to land at Lethem on the Takutu River; it will look just so on their radar.' He pushed forward on the yoke and the plane swooped down until the jungle seemed to be stretching just under their wings like an endless, unrolling magic carpet. Flights of startled rainbow-colored birds took screeching, panic-stricken flight as the roaring of the engine invaded their domain in the rainforested canopy.

'I am taking us a little south of the position you wanted. It is much easier for me to land upwind and against the current,' Gomes explained as Garibaldi glanced at the slightly veering compass bearing.

'Fine.' The priest nodded, putting his hand into the right pocket of his Vietnam-era ripstop jungle jacket, wrapping his fingers around the small object there. Garibaldi spotted the widening course of the Xingu and a mile or two ahead he could see the green ledges and the cascades of the Garden of Babylon, just as Grayle had shown him in his copy of the Fawcett notebooks.

Roughly ten minutes later Gomes brought the old floatplane down in the center of the river and slowed the engine so that it had just enough power to slowly cruise upriver toward the waterfall.

'There is the place where your friends await you,' said Gomes, nodding at a muddy beach two hundred yards away. He steered the Cessna toward the starboard bank.

As he did so Garibaldi took the already prepared Biojector from the pocket of his jacket and jammed it against the pilot's carotid. There was a hiss of CO_2 as two hundred milligrams of Zemuron was injected into the man's bloodstream. The drug, usually administered in much smaller doses, was a paralytic used in delicate surgery where mechanical breathing is required.

Gomes was paralysed instantly, and when Garibaldi pushed him out the pilot's-side door, every muscle in his body had been immobilized, although he was still fully conscious. He slipped into the river, eyes staring and mouth wide open. Either the drug overdose would kill him, he would drown or something unpleasant in the river would eat him. Garibaldi didn't care which. He had his escape plan and he had the plane. He took over the copilot's controls and guided the aircraft to the muddy shore.

14

Reaching the other side of the Xingu and hiding their boats once again, Holliday and the others were astounded to discover a set of broad steps leading upward beside the cascading waterfall. The steps had been hidden from the eastern side by an overgrowth of brush and vines, but it was easy enough to cut through with their machetes. Beside the steps in a man-made V-shaped cut in the earth, logs, now rotted with age, had been placed in the ground. At the top of the steps, they found the rusted remains of an iron hand-cranked winch and a long rusted chain.

'The crafty old devil,' said Rafi. 'He never did follow the eastern trail from the falls; he came and made a portage here with the winch.'

'What about the steps?' Holliday asked. 'Fawcett didn't make them – that's for sure – and neither did the Indians around here.'

'The Templars?' Eddie suggested.

Rafi cleared away a patch of moss at the top step, revealing a symbol carved deeply into the stone:

'Looks like one of those doodles you made on your notebooks when you were a kid,' said Peggy. 'There was usually a bunch of other doodles figuring out a neat logo using your initials.'

'It's the Phoenician symbol for Venus,' said Rafi.

'You're saying the Phoenicians were here before the Templars?' Holliday asked. 'Is that possible?'

'Why not?' Rafi shrugged. 'The Phoenicians were the ones who invented celestial navigation, after all, so they had the skills to reach South America. They also had huge ocean-going ships, and bear in mind that it was the Phoenicians who built the original Temple for Solomon.'

'So maybe it was the Phoenicians who sailed up the river first, built the steps . . . and Fawcett found them.'

'There's not a word about it in the journals, though,' Rafi said.

'Secrets within secrets,' Holliday muttered, the truth finally dawning. 'I don't think anyone paid Percy Fawcett – I think he was a member of the White Gloves himself.'

'But what about your famous Templars?' Eddie asked. 'Why did they come here?'

'The famous *Santo Antonio de Padua*, the *Santo Ovidio de Braga* and the *Santo João de Deus*. With their holds full of loot,' said Peggy. 'I thought we dumped that theory.'

'I'm starting to think it was the right one all along,' said Holliday. 'The Templar ships came up the Xingu to take something away, not bring it. Something the Phoenicians had carried here almost three thousand years before the Templars even existed.'

The theory was borne out three days later, after they'd made their way through the relentlessly noisy rainforest jungle on the eastern side of the Xingu River. Eddie's eagle eye caught a strangely even disruption in the current about a mile above a set of steep rapids, and further investigation by Rafi identified it as a roadway just under the surface. The road went from one side of the river to the other and was thirty feet wide.

'Amazing,' marveled Rafi, standing ankle-deep in the water. 'The stone is quarried and each one is held together with a dovetail joint. There's even an upstream cutwater beveled into the stone so the water flows evenly over it. This was meant to last.'

'Phoenician again?' Holliday asked.

'Without a doubt.' Rafi nodded. 'The locals couldn't have done this; they're barely out of the Stone Age now, and their focus was always nature, not empire building.'

'God bless 'em,' said Peggy under her breath. 'The stones have evenly placed runnels carved into their upper surfaces, probably to keep some kind of wheeled cart or something steady as it crossed the river. What would you want a wheeled vehicle in the jungle for?'

'I don't even want to think about it,' said Holliday.

'Neither do I,' said Rafi.

'You think it's the Ark of the Covenant, don't you?' Peggy said.

'Why did you have to say that?' Rafi asked with mock sadness. 'It's not what an archaeologist is supposed to think of. An archaeologist is supposed to be objective and not mix emotions in with his work.'

'Bullshit,' said Peggy. 'Why on earth would the Phoenicians, who had a religion with more gods and goddesses than the Egyptians, carry the Ark of the Covenant across an unknown ocean for a man who wasn't even their own king?'

'Money, of course,' called Rafi. He had walked out on to the road until he was midway across the river. 'The Phoenicians were merchants above anything else.' He bent down and examined something at his feet, then pointed to the northeast. 'There's an arrow carved into the stone; I think I know exactly where they were going.'

Holliday's gaze followed Rafi's pointing finger. In the distance, at least fifty or seventy-five miles away, a cliff-sided tabletop mountain thrust up out of the surrounding rainforest. A *tepui* as it was called in the ancient language here: 'House of the Gods.'

Roraima, Professor Challenger, *The Lost World* of Arthur Conan Doyle's imagination, fueled by Percy Fawcett's early expeditions. A place where prehistoric creatures still roamed, where giant dragonflies like *Meganeuropsis permiana* still thrived. 'Sweet Jesus,' breathed Holliday. 'It was all true.'

Cardinal Arturo Ruffino, attired in his favorite silk dressing gown, sat at the breakfast table in his luxury apartment looking down on the Piazza di Spagna, 'the Spanish Steps,' while Vittorio Monti, his lover and the head of the Vatican Secret Service, wearing his boxer shorts and an undershirt, stood at the stove and made scrambled eggs and bacon to go with the *cornetti* and the strong Italian coffee already on the table.

Ruffino folded his copy of *La Repubblica* and set the newspaper down beside his coffee. The two men had been lovers for many years, but the cardinal always felt a deep and very powerful sense of 'rightness' to their relationship. It defied the Holy Father, it defied the doctrines of the Church, it defied the holy scriptures and it defied God, but between them, two men supposedly given the gift of free will, it was the way the cardinal wanted to feel.

There was more intimacy for him in his moments with Vittorio, even simple, innocent moments like this, than he had ever felt receiving or giving the Sacrament. Even thinking such a thing would send him to the innermost circle of hell and damnation, but at this stage in his life he wasn't sure he believed in the hell and brimstone of Revelation any more than he believed in Jesus' paradise with its many mansions.

Sometimes hell was a mansion like the Vatican, disposed to the most sordid conspiracies, betrayals and even murders, and sometimes paradise was breakfast with Vittorio.

In the end, of course, it was the cardinal who destroyed his small paradise. He watched as the priest lifted the eggs on to waiting plates, added generous portions of bacon and then sat down. Monti poured more coffee for them both, then tore a flaky *cornetto* in half and slathered each piece with butter and the tart fig balsamic jam both men enjoyed so much.

'How bad is it?' Ruffino asked.

'Worse than we could have imagined,' answered Monti.

'Who?'

'Just about all of them,' the head of the Vatican Secret Service responded. He chewed on a piece of the Italian-made croissant, then gently licked a spot of jam from the corner of his mouth. Ruffino found the action almost violently erotic, but he pulled his

mind back from prurience and into the more perfidi-
ous world of Vatican finances.

'Neri, Abanndando, the fat little archbishop who
plays the stock market too much for his own good,
Mancini, who's up to his neck in it. Even Lamberto.
The only way for them to recover is to pray that White
Horse completes the dam so the diamond and mineral
holdings can be used on all the alluvial soil exposed
by the draining of all the tributaries to the river.'

'As chairman of the bank, you would think, Lamberto might have learned his lesson after the Assassini
hung Roberto Calvi from Blackfriars Bridge.'

'I don't think a wholesale lynching from the Ponte
Sisto would be useful. The Holy Father would never
live it down.' Monti smiled, putting more jam on his
cornetto.

'What about your man tracking Holliday?'

'The miniature GPS tracker we implanted while
he was at Ramstein is working perfectly,' said Monti.
'Our man as you call him knows exactly where he is.'

'When the time comes will he be able to do the
job?' Ruffino asked.

The innocent, angelic look of his friend and lover
lifted for a moment and the cardinal saw something
else for a fleeting instant.

'He would put a bullet through the Holy Father's
brain if I ordered it.'

*

Francisco Garibaldi checked the signal coming from Holliday, then referred to the waterproof topographic map in his hand. He looked up again, nodded to himself, then took the satellite phone out of its holster. 'I know where they're going. Send the help you offered to coordinates twenty-six-nine by thirty-four-seven for pickup. I should be there in an hour.'

15

Holliday stood at the foot of the enormous cliff and stared upward. The top of the *tepui* was at least a mile above him, and there was only vegetation clinging to the mountain wall for the first two or three hundred feet. Beyond that it was an unclimbable fortress.

'Why wasn't there a word about this place in Fawcett's notebooks?' Rafi asked, astonished.

'That is easy enough to answer,' said Eddie, staring up at the mountain. 'He did not want anyone who read them to know that this was his final destination.'

'I presume there's a way up to the top,' said Peggy.

'There is,' said Tanaki. 'But I cannot take you.'

'Why not?' Holliday asked.

'This is the Montanha de Deus, the Mountain of God. It is taboo to our people. My grandfather and I will show you the cave and la Garganta do Diablo. From there you must find your own way.'

'La Garganta do Diablo?' Peggy asked.

'The Devil's Throat,' translated Tanaki.

'What on earth is that?' Rafi asked.

'You will see, I am afraid,' the Indian replied ominously.

The *tepui* was enormous, not only in height but also in its circumference. According to Tanaki it was almost thirty miles around – an upthrust of Precambrian quartzite more than three billion years old. The only fossils it contained were single-celled entities and single proteins. The stone they were walking past literally represented life at the very beginning of life, and had seen a billion species come and go. The *tepuis* had been here before the oldest organism climbed out of the primordial ooze, and even predated the ooze itself.

It took more than another hour of trekking around the perimeter of the mountain before they reached the entrance to a cavern unlike any of them had ever seen before.

'*Caca Santa!*' Eddie breathed.

'No kidding,' whispered Peggy, looking up toward the roof of the cave. Even the entrance was beyond cathedral-like proportions, a towering arch four or five hundred feet high and a football field across. The cave itself was twenty times that wide and the roof, barely visible, must have been two thousand feet above them. The cave was easily large enough to land several helicopters, and at the far end of the unbelievably large space, a waterfall dropped down out of the darkness, the water's nearly mile-high fall turning to a silken mist when it hit the cavern floor, feeding a chain of small black-colored lakes joined together like pearls on a string by a wide bubbling stream.

'Notice anything?' Holliday asked.

'No bats, no stalactites or stalagmites,' said Rafi. 'The waterfall looks pure enough, but there's something in it that turns it black. That can't be healthy. It usually means high concentrations of sulfur. And notice that the vegetation stops right at the entrance. No sunlight, no photosynthesis. There weren't even a few birds flying in and out. This place is dead.'

'*Una caverna de fantasma,*' said Eddie. 'A cave of ghosts.'

'Well, one thing's clear,' said Peggy. 'Our giant dragonfly didn't come from here.'

'Where is the Devil's Throat?' Holliday asked, turning to Tanaki. The young man conferred with his grandfather. Nenderu, leaning on a long stave he'd cut for himself in the past few days, led the way. They walked along the perimeter of the cave for a thousand feet or so, bypassing huge, sharp-edged boulders and long tongues of scree that had fallen from the roof of the cave unknown millions of years ago.

Nenderu pointed with his stave.

'There,' said Tanaki, pointing to yet another pile of rocks and boulders. 'Up there.'

They climbed toward a dark shadow that seemed

to run the entire height of the cave. As she stepped closer, Peggy's eyes widened. 'That's the way up? Not a chance.'

'It is your only chance, I am afraid,' Tanaki answered. The way up was a narrow cleft or 'chimney' in the rock. It had been pegged with narrow slabs of rock pushed into deeply chiseled cracks in the walls of the crevice, and where there were no pegs there were rickety lengths of stairs between them.

The whole thing looked like a single curling strand of DNA going up into black nothingness. Every few steps there seemed to be a squared-off niche cut into the stone. At the base of the pool was a bubbling pool of bright yellow mud. The smell was foul, like dozens of rotten eggs.

'Sulfur dioxide,' said Rafi, looking down at the bubbling, rotting mess.

'The Devil has this acid reflux you see on television, I think,' said Eddie.

'We don't have to climb that today, do we?' Peggy asked.

'No, it's almost sunset. We'll camp in the cave tonight and start up first thing tomorrow.'

'When we're climbing, is there any way to avoid the smell?' Peggy asked.

'Climb as fast as you can,' said Holliday.

*

Lord Adrian Grayle, CEO of White Horse Resources and present grand master of the White Glove, sat in his office on the top floor of the Gherkin, the vibrator-shaped skyscraper at 30 St Mary Axe in London. At that moment he was in the midst of a closed-circuit video conference with Leo Krall, the head of Jericho Defense Alternatives, White Horse's security division, in its large, bunkerlike facility in the sub-basement of the building. The screen he was using was an enormous black rectangle built into the wall of his office opposite his desk.

'So, what are we dealing with?' Grayle asked.

'It looks like some concentrated effort against the dam,' said Krall, wearing the simple dark blue uniform of the JDA. Krall was in his late fifties, square-faced, lean and with hair the color of streaked granite.

'Show me,' instructed Grayle.

The huge screen instantly switched from a near-life-sized figure of Krall to a satellite image of northeastern Amazonia Province. It zoomed in on a large area of bright green with one fist-sized patch of red in the center right. Striations of dark blue ran through the entire frame of the image like tiny blood vessels leading into larger veins.

'What am I looking at?'

'An infrared image of the area about fifty miles from the dam site,' said Krall.

'The red are the Indians.'

'Yes, sir.'

'How many?'

'Approximately three hundred, sir.'

'Excellent.'

'And our personnel at the dam?'

'Evacuate them.'

'The Indians in those kinds of numbers could do a great deal of damage, sir.'

'I should bloody well hope so, Krall. That's the whole point, after all.'

Yachay, leader of his people, was leading them and four hundred other warriors of the river tribes north to defeat the gray monster. He knew this was the right thing to do from his *xhenhet* vision and had convinced the other shamans in the villages he passed through to reach his destination. Within six days of travel he had every warrior the river tribes could offer, and on the seventh day they reached their quarry and stood looking in awe at the monster from the very edge of the forest. They had seen no place and no thing like it.

'What is this place?' asked Taroya, a Munduruku whose tribe had migrated north many seasons before.

'It is the place of the beast, the monster.' Beyond the edge of the forest, the jungle had been stripped down to its sandy soil, the roots of every tree torn out of the ground like rotten teeth. The trees were piled in huge pyres that were burned for days, signal fires to the death of the forest. Littered over the barren landscape were dozens of gigantic earthmovers, scrapers and giant dump trucks on wheels the height of a grown man, and through it all ran a wide muddy stream – the source of the river that gave these men life. Beyond all this in the far distance was the monster itself, a great gray slab of concrete eight hundred feet high that ran the width of the Xingu Valley from one side to the other.

'We cannot defeat these things,' said Taroya. 'We have only blowpipes and bows and arrows and our spears.'

'We can do it,' said Yachay. 'I know this because I have seen it in my vision, and my vision is the future.' Yachay paused, staring out at the desolation. 'But my vision says we must wait for the rain and wait for the night, and that is what we shall do.'

They gathered by the Devil's Throat just as the sun began to rise over the rainforest canopy. Birds outside in the dense jungle were coming into full song, and once again the forest was alive.

'Let's get this done,' said Peggy. 'The longer we wait, the more nervous I get.'

'My grandfather says we must wait. He knows this place,' Tanaki said. 'He also asks if you will step back a few feet.'

'Why?' Peggy asked stubbornly.

In response there was a low rumbling from deep beneath the ground under their feet. It continued for at least a minute, and then the sulfur pool at the foot of the rock chimney seemed to begin boiling.

'What the hell . . . ?'

A gout of ulcerous mud rose fifty feet into the air, steam hissing as it shot up. There was a deeper-rooted explosion under their feet and the sulfur mud became white-hot steam that rose higher and higher within the chamber and then only a few seconds later subsided. The superior pool subsided and there was no sign that anything had happened.

'We would have been killed,' said Rafi.

'My grandfather says you must wait for the steps to cool and to dry before you begin to climb.'

'Does it happen regularly?' Holliday asked, thinking of Old Faithful.

'There is no way to tell,' said Tanaki.

'So either we stay here or we take our chances,' said Holliday. He thought for a moment. 'You don't have to follow, but I'm going up to the top.'

'I will come with you, *compadre*,' said Eddie. 'Our fates are bound, I think, my friend.'

'Glad to have the company.' Holliday grinned.

'Well, you're not leaving us behind,' said Peggy, taking Rafi's hand in hers.

Nenderu had a brief conversation with his grandson, and Tanaki translated. 'My grandfather will lead you,' he said. 'He can think of no better place to die than seeking entrance to the heavens, and if not that, he would very much like to see where the gods live. It is forbidden for me to go with you. I will wait for your return here.'

The climb went without incident, except for Peggy's complaints about becoming hard-boiled like eggs in a pot. The ascent took more than an hour and their lungs were aching when they reached the surface.

'What the hell?' said Holliday, looking around. They seemed to have come up into a formal, well-tended garden of paths and beds of flowers interspersed with fruit trees. The air smelled of blossoms, and the trees surrounding the gardens swayed slightly in a gentle breeze.

'*El Jardín del Edén,*' whispered Eddie.

Nenderu fell to his knees and began to chant as a man came out of the surrounding forest and approached. The man was quite short with curly hair flowing past his shoulders and a long, dark and well-oiled beard. He wore a twisted quoit of fabric around his head and a long robe studded with gems. He stopped in front of the group and bowed. He straightened, put his palms together and introduced himself. When he spoke it was in perfect English with the heavy accents of Spain, even though it was clear that he was not a native of either country.

'Welcome. I am Hiram, king of Tyre and all Phoenicia, the one hundred and twentieth of that name.'

16

Vincent Lamberto sat in his office in the Telecom Italia building and looked out at the distant skyline of Rome. His position as head of Romacorp, the largest multinational in the country, his close personal friendship with the Holy Father and his recent investiture in the Order of St Sebastian all made him the perfect candidate for the chairmanship of the Vatican Bank.

There was only one problem – Vincent Lamberto was broke. Between his attempted takeover of White Horse and the convulsions of the European monetary systems, he was spread so thin that the slightest downtick in the world markets would put him over the edge.

For the last year Romacorp had been flying on fumes in what was actually a giant Ponzi scheme that was going to have Lamberto's head on a stick when the structure went into its inevitable collapse. To make matters even worse, for the past year he'd borrowed vast amounts of money from P2, the fascist Catholic organization born out of the Second World War and now the biggest thing in European organized crime. It was a nightmare and Lamberto could see no chance of awakening from it.

Except to run. He had two hundred million euros in a Swiss account and a complete alternative identity waiting for him in a safe-deposit box. It would mean leaving his wife, children and mistress behind to take the fury that would come down on the name of Lamberto, but so be it. His wife had given him three children who whined like infants into their thirties, two of whom still lived at home. He was a sixty-five-year-old man who still had some time left to enjoy life, and a lot of life could be enjoyed on two hundred million euros in some country like Brazil, which had no extradition treaty with Italy.

Captain James Calthrop, Royal Marines Third Commando Unit (retired), landed at Fiumincino Airport and took a taxi to the Cavalieri Hotel, where Constantine had made reservations for him. Contrary to fiction, men in his occupation always preferred a large anonymous hotel over a romantic pension tucked away in some side street. For one thing the pension usually had bedbugs or roaches and it didn't have room service. There was obscurity in numbers, and as his old colonel used to say, 'Better to lie in a field of thin stalks of grass than to hide behind a single tree.'

He arrived at the hotel, signed in and went upstairs.

He swiftly unpacked his one small bag, then showered. That done, he enjoyed a room service lunch of carpaccio di manzo con la sua salsa, gazpacho andaluso and risotto ai frutti di mare followed by tiramisu and strong black coffee.

Constantine arrived exactly at two thirty. Calthrop had ordered coffee for two, knowing the tall slender man's penchant for punctuality, so there was plenty for both of them. Calthrop had worked with Constantine on several previous occasions, but he'd never got a read on the man other than a certain ascetic aura that could have been something in the man's background or a flat affect during their meetings to further his need for privacy. It didn't really matter to Calthrop and he'd long ago accepted the man for what he said he was – a middleman between Calthrop and those who required his services.

Calthrop was equally vague about himself. He always flew out of his home in the Bahamas via some other country, traveled on a Canadian passport and as chance would have it he spoke Italian like a native after spending three years in Florence getting a completely useless degree in art history for no other reason than obscuring his real origins. He'd even picked up a package of Yesmoke cigarettes at the airport instead of smoking his own Senior Service brand. In the twenty-first century, anonymity was a rare commodity and something to be protected and valued.

Constantine sat down in one of the two armchairs set beside the panoramic view of the city from the glass balcony doors. 'Mr Calthrop.' Constantine nodded, speaking in Italian.

'Mr Constantine,' answered Calthrop in the same language.

'You read the file I sent you?'

'Of course.'

'What's your opinion?'

'A powerful man with powerful friends. Allied with P2, a group his father had been involved with shortly after the war.'

'How would you do it?'

'Find out about his daily movements. The usual way – a single shot from a distance, an explosive bullet or a fléchette. He has no real security except for his driver and a single bodyguard.'

'I'm afraid we don't have that sort of luxury with this target. We have it on good authority that he's fleeing his debts via Switzerland. He's flying out tomorrow evening on a Swiss European flight into Zurich. And there can be no use of a bullet; it must look like an accident or at the very least a suicide.'

'Suicides are complicated, accidents even more so,' said Calthrop. He took out a cigarette and lit it.

'He's probably heading for Brazil if that helps.'

'Presumably because they have no extradition treaty with Italy.'

'We're assuming that, yes.'

'It's going to increase costs considerably.'

'Your fee? That can be dealt with.'

'It's going to increase other costs. I may need to make purchases, employ watchers. You've just made the project much more difficult.'

'Not by choice.'

'You want something else,' said Calthrop, looking directly into Constantine's eyes.

'Yes,' the man calling himself Constantine said. There was no point in lying. 'We need to recover two hundred million euros from this man. He may also be carrying documents, either in written or electronic form. First of all, you must retrieve those documents.'

'And the money?' Calthrop asked.

'He will have wired it to whatever his eventual destination is. Before he . . . is dealt with, you must find out where it has gone and into what account.'

'A bonus will be required.'

'Fifteen per cent.'

'Thirty,' said Calthrop.

'Twenty-five,' replied Constantine.

'Agreed.'

'So, you'll take the job?'

'I have to think about it. Give me one hour and then call me.'

'Time is of the essence here,' said Constantine.

'An hour,' repeated Calthrop firmly. 'I'll give you your answer then.'

Constantine left the suite and Calthrop poured himself another cup of coffee. The Italian never showed any hint of emotion, but this afternoon Calthrop had sensed evasion. Calthrop had completed eight projects for Constantine, all without any problem, but somehow this was different. There had been a note of finality in the austere-looking man's face, and Calthrop had an idea why. This one was personal and even when it was resolved, there could be nothing to connect Constantine to it.

So there would be a ghost, a killer watching a killer, and when it was over Calthrop would die. But Calthrop had dealt with ghosts before, and this time Constantine or whoever he was would be severely punished for his lack of trust. An hour later Constantine called and Calthrop gave him his simple answer.

'Yes.'

The man calling himself Hiram, king of Tyre and all Phoenicia, led them through what could only be described as a small paradise. There were flowering trees and plants turning the air into fragrant perfume, orchards of exotic fruits such as pomegranates and tamarind and meandering crystal streams and pools that were almost dreamlike.

There was no way that any of it was likely to be seen from the air or by satellite since the whole area was surrounded by canopy forest that allowed full light on to the gardens for only a few minutes each day. At most times the shadows cast by the huge trees would disguise the natural treasure far below them.

'Your English is very good,' said Holliday, walking beside the regally dressed man.

'I had a good teacher,' answered Hiram. 'All of us did. It's the language of this place and has been for almost a hundred years.'

'All of you?'

'Yes, we are a nation in the skies and I am its king. It has always been so.'

They walked through the gardens until they finally reached a large outcropping of rock, which, as they neared it, Holliday saw was actually the artificially hidden entrance to a narrow cave. Entering the opening behind Hiram, Holliday saw that even the cavern was artificial and clearly hewn out of the stone by human hands.

At the far end of the tunnel-like structure, there was a wide circular staircase descending into the ground. As they began to go down the steps in single file, Holliday saw that the stairway was eerily lit by natural light coming from narrow carved slots in the rock wall.

Perhaps thirty or forty feet down, the stairway

opened up and to left and right in a long curve were actual cobbled streets and rows of buildings, some made of stone and others of sand-colored brick. It was a city buried beneath the surface of the sheer mountain, the streets thronged with people – men, women and children going about their business, all dressed in simple skirtlike tunics.

'This is magnificent,' said Rafi. 'A modern Machu Picchu. A city underground cut off from the rest of the world.'

'But how is it possible?' Holliday asked. 'How do you keep an economy running, feed these people, get them medical help?'

'We are not as cut off from the world of men as you might think. And we have resources,' said the so-called king.

'What you have are mysteries,' said Holliday. 'How did you get here? Why did you come in the first place?'

'All your questions will soon be answered,' said Hiram.

They went down another five levels until, by Holliday's rough estimation, they were close to the level of the jungle at the base of the strange mountain. All the way down, both the levels of the hidden city and the staircase joining them were lit by the strangely filtered natural light. By Holliday's estimation, there was room enough for more than a thousand people in the city, and if those he had already seen were any indication, they were neither Middle Eastern nor any other race he had ever seen.

Their skin was a beautiful golden brown, like heavily creamed coffee, and their hair was mostly straight and as black as the local *indios'*. Their features were fine, neither Caucasian, Negroid nor anything else. Hiram's eyes were bright blue, which seemed strange for what would now be a Palestinian, but Holliday had seen blue, brown and black on the way down to the last level.

The bottom level of the city seemed much brighter than the others, and stepping out on to a broad cobbled street, Holliday soon saw why. Hiram led him down the street to a wide set of steps that ran down into what looked like a massive circular gorge at least a mile across, its top opening up to the blue sky high overhead.

Looking outward, he could see across to the rock wall on the far side, and in the interior there was the incredible vision of what could only be described as a jungle as it might have existed a million years or more ago. Gigantic ferns battled strange flowering trees for light, and cascading foliage of plants and vines with tentacle-like leaves flowed down the rock walls.

Holliday saw what looked like something half reptile and half bird in a fluttering flight from tree to tree, and he saw what looked like a miniature dinosaur racing across his line of vision, head high, running upright, his short front legs ending in razor claws. Out of the corner of his eye, Holliday saw something glittering and turning. He saw that it was an emerald the size of a baby's fist still in the rock matrix of the wall.

A man stepped out of the jungle to their left. He looked to be in his early to mid-thirties and was dressed like a model for Tilley Endurables complete with heavy mountaineering boots. He was wearing modern-looking aviator-style sunglasses and had a camera slung around his neck.

'That's a Hasselblad H4D-60,' whispered Peggy. 'Forty grand on the hoof. Who the hell is this guy?'

'Hello there,' he said, the accent definitely British. 'My name's Harrison Fawcett. Who might you people be?'

17

Fawcett and Hiram led the others back inside the city. Directly in front of them was a large building carved out of the rock, three stories high, its facade studded with high windows set with wooden shutters. A set of steps led into the cool interior of the building, where Hiram showed them into a large room on the left side of the broad entranceway, its surface set with a mosaic of colored stones in a design of three large sailing ships around a dark blue circular sea. In the corners of the immense mosaic, dolphins arched into the air and giant serpents twisted around the perimeter framing the whole design.

The room Hiram led them to was high ceilinged, the walls were covered in pale brick and the furniture — tables, chairs and a single large cupboard — was all wood and had brightly colored simple Mediterranean lines. The chair seats and backs were pale rattan or split bamboo and the larger seats, looking almost Egyptian in their designs, were slung with some white, closely woven cloth. There were mats and rugs of the same white fabric littered across the floor. Hiram indicated that they should sit in the larger chairs, which they did.

'Harrison Fawcett,' said Holliday. 'Let me guess, Jack's grandson?'

'That's right,' said the younger man. 'You still haven't told me your names.'

'My name is John Holliday, the young lady is my cousin Peggy, the man with the curly hair is Rafi, her husband, and this is Eddie, my good friend from Cuba.'

'I see one of the Old Ones has come with you up the Devil's Throat,' said Hiram. 'No doubt he will find some of his friends who have come before him.' Seated in the large chair, his head high and his posture straight as a statue's, he certainly did look very kinglike.

'Old Ones?'

'In the time of the first Hiram they were called magi. Harrison tells me the English word is shaman. Those with the strength sometimes come here to die. We care for them until they do.'

'His name is Nenderu,' said Holliday. 'His grandson remained behind.'

'It's taboo for any young warriors to climb here before their time,' said Fawcett.

'I have a thousand questions,' said Rafi eagerly. 'We all do, I think. Why the Phoenicians? How did they get here and why? And how does Percy Fawcett wind up with a great-grandson living in the Brazilian rainforest?'

'All your questions will be answered,' Hiram said. 'But first we must eat.'

The food was brought into the room and laid out on the table by two men and a woman a little younger than Harrison Fawcett. Holliday assumed by their uniform-like white tunics that they were servants and wondered if the old Phoenician tradition of slavery was still carried on here.

There were several courses: an enormous fish that looked like a gigantic trout, some sort of roasted fowl and slabs of succulent white meat crusted with some sort of crushed and roasted nut and a dessert of mixed fruits and dripping squares of honeycomb.

Fawcett described the dinner laid out before them, all of which turned out to be excellent. 'The big fish is called a taimen, a prehistoric version of the trout and the largest salmonid ever discovered, the bird is Brazilian shamo – something like the guinea fowl, only much larger – and the white meat is smoked tapir.'

Surprisingly, at the end of the meal, they were served rich aromatic coffee in high-sided hand-sized bowls. 'Coffee grows all over the summit,' explained Fawcett.

'Okay,' said Holliday. 'Percy Fawcett and your grandfather Jack were supposed to be a thousand miles south of here when they vanished, never to be heard from again except for various sightings for more than ten years after they vanished. What really happened?'

Fawcett smiled and sipped his coffee, gathering his thoughts. 'From what I can gather from my grandfather's stories, Percy had heard stories about this place from his previous expeditions and he believed them. On his final expedition his whole intention was to hide his true destination from everyone except his backers.'

'The White Gloves,' said Holliday.

'You've done your research, haven't you? Yes, the White Gloves, really what remained of the Order of Templars. On his previous expedition Percy had come back with some large gems from the Xingu area as well as a number of Phoenician gold coins.'

'That was enough to convince this White Glove organization?'

'According to my grandfather they had their own sources of information. He just provided the concrete proof.'

'You spoke as if you knew your grandfather well. How old was he when he died?'

'He lived here for many years. He was a hundred and nine when he died.'

'Amazing,' said Rafi.

'Not so amazing.' Fawcett shrugged. 'I'm fifty-two, for instance, and Hiram is well into his eighties. It seems that living here has a beneficial effect on one's health.' He shrugged again. 'No one is really sure, but I think it's the concentrated oxygen levels down here on the bottom of the mountain.'

'The giant dragonfly we found in Raleigh Miller's box,' said Peggy.

'The dragonfly he stole, not to mention Percy's notebooks,' said Fawcett. 'They found the dragonfly dead a few miles away from the mountain. Percy mounted it and that night Raleigh disappeared along with the notebooks.'

'And that's the end of the story?' Holliday asked.

'For Percy it was. He'd contracted some sort of infection along the way, and no matter what, they couldn't cure him here. Somehow from what my grandfather told me he was just as happy to die here. He saw the great wealth this wonderful place represents and he knew the Glove would only destroy it to enrich themselves. The people here would not have survived. He's buried on the summit, facing the sunrise, which was his dying wish.'

'How do you figure in all of this?'

'Jack, my grandfather, married one of the local women. They had a child. He was named Percy, in honor of his grandfather. His namesake had been a great believer in education, so when my father was eighteen Grandfather Jack took him up the Essequibo River to Georgetown, where he sold a handful of gems for cash and held back a bag of even finer stones for his son's use abroad.

'He bought young Percy a fake American passport and put him on a freighter for the United States. This was shortly after the end of the war. Percy wrote the entrance examinations at Harvard University and ten years later emerged as a medical doctor, paying his tuition and expenses using the second bag of stones.

'Dr "Smith" returned here with his knowledge and an assortment of useful medical supplies. That was in 1957. I made my own trip in 1976, to Cambridge this time, using a counterfeit British passport. Eight years later I had an official passport and degrees in paleontology and prehistoric botany. I've been cataloging the flora and fauna here ever since and I've barely begun.'

'Do you ever leave the mountain?' Holliday asked.

'Regularly. The same route my father and grandfather made. From Georgetown I go either to America or the United Kingdom for supplies and books, then bring them back to Georgetown. I keep a boat there and hide it carefully at the end of the journey. I have a prearranged return date and my people meet me at the boat and help me bring the supplies back to the mountain. Soon I will be sending the first of my sons on his own journey.'

'You have children?' Rafi asked.

'Three sons and two daughters. Each will make the journey into the outside world when they feel they're ready. For all King Hiram's royal stature, he deals far more in ecclesiastical matters than those of day-to-day living. The mountain is essentially a democracy, each level electing two members to sit on what they call the Great Council.'

'What's your role in all of this?' Holliday asked.

Fawcett smiled and shrugged. 'Adviser, teacher of children, librarian, a botanist who tells the people here which creatures and plants in the canyon are beneficial and which are dangerous. A medical doctor or what passes for it with the help of my father's textbooks, a midwife when it is required. A jack-of-all-trades and master of a few.' Fawcett's expression darkened. 'I'm also a man who keeps his ear to the ground for any information about activities that might harm this place.'

'Such as?'

'Such as I am aware that what is nothing more than the modern-day version of the Glove is building a dam nearby. It purports to be for power generation, but its real intent is to dry out the downriver plain to expose the ancient alluvial river courses that ran through the valley. They've already got a test mine for diamonds, and when the dam is complete it will have accomplished two things – destroyed the hunting and fishing habitats of the river people and provided a trail back to the source of the gems – this mountain.'

'You're talking about White Horse,' Holliday said.

'And the present Lord Grayle, the direct descendant of the man who underwrote Percy Fawcett's last expedition. They knew something then, and they know more about this place now. I can't allow them to destroy what this place has become and what it once was.'

'Cryptic,' Holliday said. 'But how are you going to stop them?'

'There's a band of warriors on the way there now.'

'What do you propose doing?'

'I'm going to help them blow the dam to hell and gone.'

18

'May I ask a question?' Rafi said, looking thoughtful.

'Of course,' said Fawcett.

'You just said, "What this place has become and what it once was." What did you mean by that?'

'I think that question is for His Majesty to answer,' said Harrison Fawcett, turning toward the king.

King Hiram nodded. 'The answer to that lies far in the past, when Solomon was king of Jerusalem. Most people credit him with the building of the Holy Temple there, but Solomon was no architect and in fact it was the Phoenicians of Tyre who designed and constructed it. Which means they also knew its secrets.'

'Where the treasure chambers were for the holy relics and what those treasures were,' said Rafi.

'And other secrets,' said Hiram. 'When the Jews were exiled to Babylon well after Solomon's time, the treasures of the temple were taken out through a passageway known only to a few. It was hidden in Tyre until the time of Herod and was then returned to the Second Temple, once again built by the architects of Tyre.

'There was secret news before the destruction by

the Romans of the Second Temple almost forty years after the death of Christ. The temple had hidden those most holy relics for almost seven hundred years, and once again they were secretly removed to Tyre, where the Romans could not find them in their attempts to wipe out Christianity. Matthew, the tautological wonder, fearing for the great relics and treasure, decreed that four ships be built of Roman design, each sixty meters long, and that the relics be divided between them. Their only instructions were to sail "beyond the Pillars of Hercules" and despite storms and the fury of the raging seas be taken to a place of safety far beyond the Romans' grasp.'

'The Pillars of Hercules,' said Holliday. 'Gibraltar.'

'Eight miles wide,' said Rafi. 'The Phoenicians were the first to chart them almost three thousand years ago.'

'And much farther. The ships sent out by the disciple Matthew had the benefit of secret charts of most of the southern Atlantic, Spain, even the African coast. When they sailed into the mouth of the Amazon, they knew exactly what they were doing,' said King Hiram.

'Is that possible?' Peggy asked.

'It's easily within the realm of possibility,' said Rafi. 'In 440 BC King Hanno of Carthage, a Phoenician protectorate, sailed a fleet as far as Sierra Leone; that much is history. From the coast of Sierra Leone to

Brazil is less than two thousand miles, an easy jump for ships weighing more than seventy-five tons. There's even evidence of Phoenician copper mining in Brazil and Mexico. The whole story could easily be true.'

'I can assure you that it is,' said Hiram.

'And the Templar ships?'

'According to my forefathers, the Templars were nothing more than brigand knights without a lord, so they created a religious order to give cause to their appearance in the place the Christians call the Holy Land. They were thieves, blackmailers and looters above all else.' The king smiled. 'According to Harrison, their descendants have changed very little over the centuries.'

'But why did they come here?' Holliday asked. 'The ship discovered by Grayle's Excalibur Marine Exploration Corporation, the *Santo Antonio de Padua*, had been full of gold coins.'

'Tyre was one of the last Crusader strongholds in what was then called the Kingdom of Jerusalem. Before it was overrun by the Mamluks in 1291, the Templars looted the city, including its archives. They found records of the voyage ordered by Matthew the Apostle and copies of the maps provided to them. Returning to France, they gave the information to their leader, Grand Master Jacques de Molay. A number of years later Molay began to see the handwriting on the wall and called in a debt from the Republic of Genoa, which was supposed to finance two ships to follow in the wake of the Phoenician expedition from hundreds of years before. They never made it, presumably ambushed by Philip of France's henchmen. Then in the latter years of the fifteenth century, three ships appeared.'

'Financed by Pedro de Menezes Portocarrero, a high-ranking naval officer and grand master of the Real Ordem dos Cavaleiros de Nosso Senhor Jesus Cristo.'

'The Templars,' said Peggy. 'We've heard this bit before.'

'They came with one ship full of gold to bribe us and two ships full of soldiers to make war with us if we refused the bribe. We refused the bribe and they tried to conquer us. It was a rout. The Devil's Throat was the only way to reach us, and they hadn't counted on our friends in the forest. It took less than a week despite their superior weapons. Of the five hundred men who attacked, four hundred and twenty died. The rest surrendered and those men's descendants still live here to this day. In two thousand years in the place, it was the only time we have ever been attacked.'

'I'm still not sure why they came here in the first place,' said Peggy.

'Because Admiral Portocarrero thought he could retrieve the holy relics and make the Templars untouchable by his enemies – popes, kings, you name it,' said Holliday.

'The same thing my grandfather's backers wanted in the Twenties,' said Harrison Fawcett. 'And the same thing Grayle wants today – power.' Fawcett paused for a moment, a dark look flashing across his features. 'There's not much in the way of Grayle's intentions, I'm afraid, but there is one fly in his particular jar of ointment.'

'Which is?' Holliday asked.

'The pope,' answered Fawcett. 'Restoring the lost relics of the Old Testament would give them enough publicity to take the sting out of the events in their recent past. Attendance in churches would skyrocket. Tours of the relics all over the world would make millions and could perhaps even ease the pressures now being felt by the Vatican Bank. They might even finally get you and their friends out of their hair – my sources tell me you've been like the proverbial thorn in their side for quite some time.'

Holliday closed his eyes and felt the soft fragrant breezes sifting in through the shuttered windows, and suddenly none of it mattered anymore. He realized that for years now he'd been following everybody else's dreams and fears, living other people's secrets and lies, and he realized how tired he was of it all.

From the day Peggy had found that hidden sword in his uncle Henry's house so long ago, his world had changed irrevocably and sent him down a rabbit hole into an underworld of conspiracies and secret societies he'd never even known were there.

If questioned, most people would tell you that the Templars had been a force for good during the Crusades and were now no more than a memory of what it meant to be loyal, truthful and kind.

The world had turned upside down – lies were truth; laws meant nothing if you had money enough to bend them or change them or just pretend they didn't exist. 'Promise' was an empty word and greed was the only god.

And here it didn't seem to matter.

That night he slept, and sleeping, dreamed; not something he did much of anymore. It was a long time ago and he was on his only real vacation. They went down the coast of the Irish Sea from Dublin and stopped in Wicklow Town. Amy was still painting then, anything that caught her incredible eye; it was as though she could see everything in anything or anyone she painted, what had made it what it was and the aura that stood around it.

On that distant afternoon they picnicked on a high hill above the town. Afterward Amy set up her folding easel and she began to paint while he dozed off, the smell of clover rich in his nostrils. Two hours later he awoke to find the watercolor almost finished.

A seascape with the ruins of the Black Castle of

Bryne, Cromwell's last conquest before taking the whole of Ireland, in the foreground and Wales a dark line of dangerous gray on the horizon. In the center was the hard, cold expanse of the Irish Sea, reflecting pewter light up into a cloudless pewter sky. To the far right of the painting, as though at the end of vision, there was a faint blue patch of sea lit by an invisible sun. He suddenly knew exactly what the painting was about:

> Attend all ye who list to hear our noble
>   England's praise
> I tell of the thrice-famous deeds she
>   wrought in ancient days,
> When that great Fleet Invincible against
>   her bore in vain
> The richest spoils of Mexico, the stoutest
>   hearts of Spain.

'The Spanish Armada,' said Holliday. 'Just before they appeared on the horizon.'

'Something like that.' She smiled.

'And you see all that?' Holliday asked.

'Doesn't everybody?' Amy smiled again.

He woke at dawn with tears streaming down his face, but his heart was fuller than he thought it could ever be again. He had not dreamed since the night of her terrible passing, and the dream he'd just had was a gift beyond words. Holliday had held her in his heart and in his mind for more than a decade now, and seeing her smile and laugh, he knew that he was whole once again and knew that death had no power over him. As Dylan Thomas said in his famous poem, 'Though Lovers be lost, Love shall not and Death shall have no dominion.'

Amy would be his forever.

Eddie, Holliday and Harrison Fawcett sat on the wide steps leading into the magical gorge at the bottom of the *tepui* known as the Mountain of the Gods and watched as in the distance King Hiram led Peggy and Rafi on a tour. Peggy was snapping pictures and Rafi was taking samples, and they both seemed completely enthralled.

'They seem very happy here,' said Holliday. 'It reminds me of *Lost Horizon*.'

'Shangri-la?' Fawcett smiled. He nodded. 'They have a lot in common. All forms of utopia have their flaws.'

'The locals all grow old as soon as they leave here?' Holliday smiled.

'Not quite that bad, but they seem to sicken greatly and are very prone to infections, especially to the lungs and upper respiratory tract.'

'The hyperoxgenated atmosphere?'

'Presumably, over the centuries the DNA of

Hiram's people, and through intermarriage, many of the other familial strains living here have mutated. It probably also has something to do with the diet, as well. The Fawcett genes are only a very recent addition, so those mutations haven't occurred in my genetic structure. It's complicated.' He paused, then smiled. 'You dreamed last night, didn't you?'

'We both did,' said Holliday.

'Good dreams?'

'The first I've had in many years. I was with my wife again. I saw her as clearly as I see you.'

'I dreamed of being a child again,' said Eddie. 'So curious, so strange. I used to run through Habana in the middle of the night with no clothes on. Everyone called me El Vampiro. I have never felt so free again.'

'This place is like that,' said Fawcett. 'Maybe it's the air or just the magic of the mountain. I've never quite known which.'

'I feel like I could stay here forever,' said Holliday. 'Perhaps then I could find peace.'

'Not if the Devil finds you first, and I'm afraid he's coming. For all of us.'

19

Francisco Neri arrived in St Gallen, Switzerland, from Zurich on board a four-passenger Eurocopter AS350 Ecureuil owned by Biomedix A.G., whose headquarters were a large white glass and steel building on the outskirts of the small northern Swiss town. St Gallen had been named after the famous monastery of St Gall, but in the twenty-first century the monastery was no more than a tourist attraction and her main economic life was provided by high-tech start-up companies like Biomedix.

A private car took him to the Biomedix headquarters at 95 Rorschacher Strasse, and ten minutes later he was sitting in the company's conference room. There were three people in white coats at the conference table with him: Dr Franz Heller, director of Project Andromeda, Dr Jurgen Wolff, head of the paleobotany division, and Dr Dragova Krilencu, evolutionary biologist and primate geneticist.

'I've come for your latest report and the documentation that comes along with it,' said Neri, getting immediately to the point.

'And the payment?' Franz Heller said, equally curt.

'I would like a simple progress report and if that is satisfactory I shall give you the funds and you will give me the full documentation,' Neri responded. 'Presumably that would be satisfactory?'

'Certainly,' said Heller. He nodded toward Jurgen Wolff, a heavyset man in his fifties with a streaked, dark beard. Wolff folded his hands across his belly and began to speak as though he were giving a lecture at a university podium.

'Yes,' said Wolff. 'So far the environment has been established as being just under two kilometers in depth with a barometric pressure that shows oxygen concentrations as being almost twice that under normal air pressure at sea level, thus in all probability ensuring the survival of the flora and fauna we have discovered in the sinkhole. It is in effect a time capsule, and such material that has risen to the surface of the *tepui* or table mountain seems to include a wide diversity of both plant and animal life that could no doubt be set in the early to mid stages of the Cretaceous period some sixty-five million years ago, give or take a million.' He paused, perhaps expecting some laughter at his little joke, and received none. Clearing his throat, Wolff went on. 'Some of the plant life includes the St Helena heliotrope, the prehistoric olive, the dwarf ebony and the dwarf cabbage tree. Thirty-eight variants of *Cinchona*, currently used in the manufacture of quinine, and one hundred and seventy-two other plants that, through examination of the DNA from the spores collected by the low-altitude scoops, show clear and exciting evidence of medicinal use.'

'Far more to the point, Signor Neri,' said Krilencu, 'is the discovery of hair follicles from the *Solimoea acrensis*, a prehistoric cousin of the spider monkey. The primate, like his modern counterpart, has a long prehensile tail for extra mobility. It also has one other asset that the modern versions lack – the ability to regenerate its limbs. As a primate, *Solimoea acrensis* has a great deal in common with human beings, and we have been able to isolate the genes that cause the regeneration.'

'Is there any proof of this?'

Krilencu reached into the left-hand pocket of her lab coat, took out a sealed petri dish and slid it across the table to Neri. Neri stared down at the table. Inside the dish was a three-quarters-grown adult thumb rising from the flesh-colored gel of the petri dish.

'The tissue was taken from a hospital patient who had lost his thumb in an industrial meat slicer,' said the woman. 'When fully grown it will be reattached. Since it is created from the man's own tissue, re-attachment will be much easier. Our next experiment shall be to regenerate an entire limb while the rest of it is still in place. This presents some serious difficulties, but we project three years before we can bring the technology to market. Given the wars, traffic accidents and other situations needing tissue replacement of one kind or another, the patent will be worth billions.'

'And the stock options should I choose to participate?'

'A six per cent bonus now and three per cent per year as well as a base block of stock at today's price, as we discussed,' said Heller.

Neri smiled. 'Then perhaps we should get down to business.'

James Calthrop, the assassin hired by 'Constantine,' sat in his rental car and watched Neri emerge from the Biomedix headquarters and climb into a black Mercedes limousine. He headed back into town and Calthrop followed. They eventually arrived at the Raddison Blu out by the autoroute leading to Lake Constance and the Austrian border. It was the town's only four-star hotel and it also included a franchised Swiss casino. According to Neri's file, his favorite games were baccarat, chemin de fer and American-style blackjack, or *vingt-et-un* as it was called in Europe.

Neri checked in at the front desk, was given a swiped key card and went up to his room, which turned out to be on the twelfth floor. Once again Calthrop followed. He watched Neri enter room 1223 and close the door behind him. Calthrop returned to the lobby and waited. Forty-five minutes later Neri reappeared in the lobby in evening dress and went into the restaurant. From there Calthrop assumed the Italian would spend at least an hour or two in the casino.

Calthrop went up to the twelfth floor, found 1223 and paused in front of the door. He felt for the small outlet at the base of the lock and plugged in the palm-sized card reader he had in his jacket pocket, and the light above the lock turned green. Calthrop opened the door, stepped inside and closed the door behind him. Like all the rooms in the hotel, Neri's was done in a décor of pale yellows and whites, the furniture all ultramodern. Calthrop fetched a bottle of Perrier from the minibar, opened it and sat down on the couch to wait. Neri might take hours to return to the room, but Calthrop didn't mind; he'd always been a patient man.

In fact, it was well past midnight before the gentle click of the lock announced Neri's return. He came into the living room already undoing his bow tie and unbuttoning his vest. Seeing Calthrop, he stopped dead in his tracks, a sudden look of both fear and desperate understanding on his face.

'*Chi diavolo siete?*' Neri blustered.

'I am an emissary from the bank,' answered Calthrop.

'What bank?'

'Don't be silly, Signor Neri. I am an emissary from the bank from which you embezzled two hundred million euros.'

'What madness are you talking about?'

'Come, come, signor, it really won't do. You know why I'm here and you know very well who sent me.'

'Assassini,' said Neri, his face draining and his voice dull. He flopped down on to an upholstered chair.

'Yes, I suppose that's who they are, although they've distanced themselves from you through a middleman, of course. They wanted me to make it look like an accident.'

'Accident?'

'Yes. All those American television dramas aside, it's quite easy to murder someone and have it look like an accident. Coroners and medical examiners are far too reliant on technology these days, which makes it even easier. Using a fine-grade needle to inject pure distilled water into the carotid in the neck or the femoral artery in the thigh gives the effect of a massive cerebral hemorrhage or stroke – certainly a possibility for a man of your general health and age.'

'Then why haven't you killed me? Do you enjoy your little game of cat and mouse? Are you some sort of sadist?'

'I thought we might have a chat,' said Calthrop. 'I've been doing a great deal of thinking about our present situation. It bears discussion.'

'What does an assassin think?'

'In this case he thinks about both his employers and the man he is employed to kill.' Calthrop paused, watching the prominent vein in Neri's forehead slow its pulsing. 'Would you like a drink, *signor*?'

'Tuaca,' said Neri.

Calthrop went to the minibar, found a bottle of the orange-brown liqueur and poured a small scoop of crushed ice into a double shot glass. He poured in the Tuaca and handed it to Neri, then sat down again. The Italian took a large swallow and gave a little sigh.

'Go on,' he said, taking a small sip.

Calthrop took out his cigarettes and offered one to Neri, who shook his head, then lit one for himself. 'There is no question who my employer is simply because you are who you are, Signor Neri. You are chairman of the Vatican Bank and as such one of the few people who is in a position to embezzle two hundred million euros from that institution. Logically that means that my employer is someone within the Vatican.'

'I can think of several,' said Neri, a slightly acid tone in his voice. 'But I fail to see your point.'

'The point is, Signor Neri, that above all else the Vatican is a business. Businesses tend to be practical and there is nothing at all practical about revenge. So why do they want you dead?'

'You speak theoretically, I suppose,' replied the

Italian, finishing his drink. He set the empty glass down on the black lacquered table beside the chair.

'Not at all,' said Calthrop. 'It makes no sense. You have the money and they know they're not going to get it back, but they did seem very interested in where it was going.'

'I don't understand.'

'Neither did I for quite some time,' said Calthrop, 'but it finally dawned on me that the money was of no interest at all. Their interest lies in you and who you're affiliated with outside of the bank.'

'I don't know what you mean.'

'What is Biomedix?' Calthrop said.

Neri looked stunned. 'How do you know about them?'

'I followed you, of course; my own life is at stake here, as well.'

'Why your life?' Neri said, perplexed.

'That should be obvious; when I discover where the money is being placed or who it is being given to, and when I report that fact to my employers, I go from being an asset to a threat. I know too much. They'll have me killed by an independent contractor who has no idea what my mission was.' Calthrop paused. When he spoke again his voice had hardened. 'Biomedix.'

'They'll kill me,' Neri said.

'And if you don't tell me I'll kill you first, and it

definitely won't look like an accident.' Calthrop reached under his jacket and took out a SIG Sauer Mosquito, a Swiss-made automatic pistol. He reached into his side pocket, took out a six-inch suppressor and screwed it on to the end of the .22's threaded barrel. In a hotel room firing the weapon would sound no louder than a champagne cork.

'Biomedix is doing research into rainforest plants and animals for potential medical use.'

'The money was given to them?'

'Yes, for a voting share, a position on the board of directors and stock options.'

'On whose instructions did you do this?'

'They'll kill me.'

Calthrop sighed. 'Let's not get on that roundabout, shall we?'

There was a long pause and then Neri spoke, the words grudging. 'Lord Adrian Grayle. White Horse Resources.'

'Were you acting on the company's orders or is this somehow connected with the White Glove?' Calthrop said.

'You know about that?'

'I am an assassin by trade, Signor Neri, not by education. I chose this job because it paid much better than being an Oxford don with several useless degrees in history. So, which was it?'

'The White Glove.'

'You are a member?'

'My family has been in the order for more than nine hundred years.'

'And why is the White Glove interested in Biomedix?'

'They're not, but part ownership will act as a cover for what they're really doing in Brazil.'

'Which is?'

'I haven't been told. Only that it's a religious arti-fact of some kind. There are rumors in the Vatican about their efforts, as well.'

'That's all you know?'

'Yes.'

'Where were you going after you left here?'

'Paris. I have a place there under the name of Nazorine. Ten Avenue Foch, St Mandé. It's hidden behind some flats. It's a house in the courtyard.'

'Why do you have it?'

'Why does any man have such a place in Paris?'

'Is there anyone occupying it now?'

'No.'

'Good,' said Calthrop. He nodded to himself, picked up the silenced pistol and shot Neri three times, twice in the chest and once in the head. Then he went out of the room and began to run the bath.

20

Calthrop had never had his fingerprints taken, but by both nature and inclination he was a careful man. He slipped a pair of surgical gloves on, then crossed the room. He emptied out the melted ice from Neri's glass into the bar sink, wiped it off with his handkerchief, then pocketed the tiny two-ounce bottle of Tuaca along with its screw top.

Calthrop then picked up Neri under the armpits and dragged him across the living room to the bathroom. The tub was a large, circular Jacuzzi style, and after five minutes it was still less than a third full. Calthrop slipped Neri into the water, then waited patiently while it filled. Eventually there was enough to cover the body and then using the index finger of his right hand, Calthrop pushed the man's head beneath the surface. The immersion would slow the decomposition process for a while, especially after he'd turned up the air-conditioning.

He went back out to the living room, picked up the telephone and called the front desk. Calling himself Francisco Neri, he asked them to add another three days to his stay and said that under no circumstances was he to be disturbed, even by housekeeping; he had a great deal of work to do and needed absolute peace and quiet.

He hung up the phone, picked up Neri's leather computer case, emptied the man's wallet of all the cash it held and left the suite, hanging the DO NOT DISTURB sign on the door lever and returning to the lobby.

In the lobby Calthrop used his cell phone to call Constantine. It was answered on the second ring.

'Constantine.'

'It's me,' said Calthrop without identifying himself.

'Is it done?'

'Yes.'

'You have the information?'

'I have the computer.'

'Excellent. When can you get it to me?'

'The day after tomorrow. Early.'

Constantine's voice was hesitant. 'Why so long?'

'There were complications.'

'What sort of complications?'

'Switzerland was a feint. He got off one plane and on to another.'

'Destination?'

'Paris. He has a pied-à-terre here under the name of Nazorine.'

'How droll,' said Constantine, his voice cold.

'It's in the St Mandé district, Ten Avenue Foch.

185

Through a porte cochère and in a courtyard, very discreet.'

'How did it happen?'

'I made it look as though he had a stroke. He was behind the wheel of a rental car. He went off the D928 on the Route de St Momelin and into the canal. A few miles outside St Omer. They haven't discovered the body or the car yet. They'll presume he was going to the ferry at Dunkirk, I'd expect.'

'Are cleaners necessary?'

'At the house in Paris?'

'Yes.'

'Only if you think he might have had something incriminating there.' Calthrop paused. 'Be that as it may, I'll be leaving by train tomorrow evening. I'll get in the following morning.'

'Why don't you just fly?'

'I don't like the idea of someone looking into the subject's computer files. It could be loaded with child pornography for all I know.'

'I see your point,' agreed Constantine. 'Come at nine.'

'Nine o'clock it is.'

Calthrop snapped the cell phone closed and smiled. Constantine would have plenty of time to get his cutout killer to Paris, but Calthrop would be waiting for him.

*

Holliday and Eddie sat at the long stone table in the main chamber of King Hiram's palace, watching Peggy and Rafi compare photographs and specimens as they sat together on the wide steps leading down into the prehistoric canyon. Out in the center of the jungle, Harrison Fawcett and King Hiram were walking along one of the narrow trails, their heads bent together in serious conversation. All around them King Hiram's people collected strange fruit from the trees and gathered the plants that grew in such profusion. Far in the distance Eddie and Holliday could see three pairs of men gathering honey from the hives that were bulging heavily from cracks in the far walls of the canyon. Birds sang and screeched, small animals chattered and there was even the burbling of a small stream running out from a pool fed by a knife blade cascading waterfall that fell from the tabletop mountain's summit.

Eddie was smoking one of his last cigars. He was frowning.

'I know what you're thinking, *compadre*,' said Holliday.

'*Tú crees?*' Eddie asked, raising one eyebrow. 'Then tell me.'

'You're thinking that this place is like the perfect idyllic scene at the beginning of a horror movie where the beautiful young native girl slips off her loincloth and dives into the water and then gets

eaten alive by a horde of hungry flesh-eating pi-
ranhas.'

'Close enough, *mi coronel*. It was the movie where
the Amazon riverboat captain is smoking in the stern
of his boat just before he goes to sleep when a
fifty-foot anaconda leaps out of the river and swal-
lows him whole.'

'But this really is paradise,' said Holliday.

Eddie sighed. 'We are too old for such dreams,
amigo. And this place gives me the . . .'

'Heebie-jeebies? Willies? Creeps?'

'The word in Cuba is *horripilante*,' said Eddie, 'but I
like your creeps much better. Like someone crossing
my grave in very cold boots.' The Cuban shook his
head. 'I have put my brain to it, but I can't see it yet,
comprendes?'

'It's like a jigsaw puzzle that was made with too few
pieces. You can't get the full picture no matter how
much you try.'

Peggy had gathered up her cameras and rushed
back up the steps and into Hiram's 'palace' or 'villa,'
depending on how you judged a house cut out of a
single piece of the native rock. Behind her Rafi was
following at a slower pace with what looked like a
small wooden box cradled in his hand.

Peggy set the camera on and pointed at the large
screen on the back. 'What does that look like?'

Holliday stared. 'A flying rat with a long beak, claws and big teeth. It looks like it's a miniature delta-wing fighter landing on a tree branch.'

'It's a *Sharovipteryx*,' said Rafi, joining Peggy at the table. 'Half reptile, half bird.' He slid back the lid of the little box. Inside was a perfect skeleton of the same type of creature Peggy had photographed. 'We saw a microraptor, as well – a two-foot-long flying lizard with feathers. It's like time just stopped down here. This is a goddamn time machine!'

They sat and talked for the better part of an hour, Holliday speaking little, letting Peggy and Rafi chatter on, allowing their enthusiasm to carry them away, watching their pure, almost childlike awe and pleasure at discovering not a lost world, but a brand-new world. They were having the time of their lives in paradise, and it wasn't paradise at all. Eventually Harrison Fawcett returned from his discussion with Hiram and sat down at the table with the others.

'You're looking very thoughtful, Colonel,' commented the lost explorer's grandson.

'I am,' murmured Holliday.

'A penny for them.' Fawcett smiled.

'Careful, my friend. You might get more than a single penny's worth,' warned Eddie.

'Why so gloomy, Doc?' Peggy asked. 'Rafi's in heaven. This place is a gift to science.'

'I haven't seen much giving going on, just a lot of secrecy. Harrison and good old King Hiram won't let you out of here with a single specimen or photograph ... if he lets any of us out of here at all.'

'Now, hold on a minute, Colonel –'

'No, you hold on a minute, Fawcett. This place is exactly what it looks like, a paleontological lost world, and you're doing just about anything to see that it stays that way. At any cost.'

'I'm trying to protect my people,' argued Fawcett.

'Which is why there's an entire tribe of indigenous river people going off to destroy the Itaqui Dam, and they're not going to do it with blowguns and spears, Fawcett. They're going to do it with explosives, which you purchased for them. You're distracting whoever's really interested in this place and for whatever reason, and you're willing to send hundreds, maybe even thousands of people to their deaths ... all for your little secret.'

'Their environment is being destroyed,' said Fawcett. 'We're on their side, and if you can't see that you're not as smart as I gave you credit for being, Colonel.'

'If they succeed, which they probably won't, their environment will be flooded instead of being parched.

One way or the other your grandfather's old friends at what they used to call the White Glove won't take it lying down. They'll firebomb or gas or murder the river people one way or the other. It's genocide no matter what you call it, and you're just as responsible, Mr Fawcett.'

'You don't know what you're talking about.'

'There's lots I don't know and I think it's time I got a few answers.'

'Then ask your questions, sir,' said Hiram, appearing in the doorway. He was dressed entirely in white with a gold-beaded belt to cinch his robes.

'Why did Raleigh Miller, who presumably was actually Raleigh Miller, Jack Fawcett's friend, run away from the expedition? Was it because he knew that escaping was the only way out from here?'

'No, it was because he killed Jack,' said Harrison Fawcett.

'Why would Miller kill him? They were good friends.'

'Because he caught Miller stealing his father's notebooks and because Jack found out he was spying for the Glove.'

'So why didn't he report back to them when he returned to England?'

'They'd promised him fame and fortune in Hollywood if he discovered where the relics were hidden, but by the time he came out of the jungle, he must have realized the truth – he was nothing to them except a witness, and the Glove did not abide witnesses to their secrets very well.'

'And there were no relics anyway; he would have been the bearer of bad news.'

'The relics are here, I assure you.'

'You're lying.' Holliday shook his head sadly. 'Logic makes you a liar.'

'What logic is that?'

'The logic that any one of your various enemies has figured out by now. The logic says that the relics commonly called the Ark of the Covenant would never be given to a Phoenician ship and sent off over the edge of the world.'

'There is concrete evidence that the Phoenicians reached the New World,' argued Fawcett.

'There may be evidence back then, but they didn't have it then. They knew that beyond the Pillars of Hercules it was anybody's guess, and you don't put the greatest relic that ever existed into a situation with odds like that.'

'So why did the Templars come?'

'I don't think one thing has anything to do with the other. I think they were looking to hide their hoard somewhere where the Catholic Church couldn't get their hands on it, and I think they died of disease. You took the survivors prisoner and simply took the gold. The whole thing is just one rumor piled on the other. It's all sleight of hand.'

'You're almost exactly right in your deductions, Colonel,' said Hiram, smiling.

'Where was I wrong?'

'There is a relic here, a very important one.'

'Show me,' said Holliday.

21

Hiram left the large, ornately decorated chamber, Fawcett going with him. Peggy glared at Holliday, and Rafi was clearly upset.

'You may have been right in some of your assumptions, Doc, but you didn't have to be so blunt about it.'

'I don't like being led around by the nose, which is how I'm beginning to feel about this whole adventure. I don't like being a pawn on somebody else's board.'

'Pawn or not,' said Peggy, 'this place is a treasure house even if there are no artifacts. This place could rewrite the book on evolution. Rafi said he's found dozens of plants and insects that no one has ever heard of. It's a time machine and an invaluable asset to science.'

'It might be if I thought they were going to make its existence public,' answered Holliday.

'He can't stop us from leaving,' said Peggy.

'I wouldn't push that too far, kiddo. They've kept this place secret for a couple of thousand years. I don't think they're going to break the pattern now.'

'If we are to leave here, it must be secretly,' advised Eddie.

'I agree,' said Holliday.

'You're both crazy,' snorted Peggy. 'These are the gentlest people in the world.'

'Said Captain Cook as he was beaten and stabbed to death by his friends the Hawaiians,' Holliday answered.

Hiram and Harrison Fawcett returned, followed by four men carrying what appeared to be an extremely heavy object on a wooden litterlike carrying device. The four men set the object down in the center of the stone table and left the room. It was a stone box, possibly limestone or granite, roughly two feet deep, three feet wide and five feet long. It was clearly very, very old.

'It's an ossuary,' said Rafi. 'Is there an inscription?'

Hiram stuck his fingers in a goblet of water and smeared it across the long side of the box facing Rafi. A faint line of lettering etched into the chalky stone appeared.

'It's Aramaic,' said the Israeli. 'Ancient Hebrew.'

Matityahu ben Yohanan HaKohen

'What does it mean?' Peggy asked.

'Mattathias ben Johanan. He was a high priest in

the first temple. He died in 169 BC. He was also the father of Judas Maccabeus, one of the great Hebrew warriors right along with Joshua, Gideon and David.'

'As in David and Goliath?'

'Yes,' Rafi answered.

'So it's not St Matthew.'

'Way before that.'

'It's interesting as a biblical artifact,' said Holliday. 'But why all the fuss? It's not Christ's bones or the Spear of Destiny or the Shroud or any of the so-called Relics of Power that people like these neo-Templars or Hitler or any loony you could name get all hot and bothered about.'

'Perhaps you are being a little quick to judge,' said Hiram mildly.

'I just don't see it,' said Holliday, 'or how the Phoenicians saw it two millennia ago, or the Templars a thousand years after that.'

'Can you remove the top?' Rafi asked.

'Certainly,' said Hiram. He gave a low whistle and the men who had borne the heavy stone box returned. He conversed with them briefly in his own language and they lifted the heavy stone lid from the ossuary and laid it down on the table. They set a thick, linen-like cloth down beside the lid.

Rafi leaned over and looked into the box's interior. 'Unbelievable,' he whispered. Holliday looked over his shoulder and Peggy lifted her camera as Hiram reached into the box. Hiram gently lifted out a bundle of what were clearly human bones and laid them on the cloth. The bundle was held together by thick gold wire at each end.

Peering into the interior of the ossuary, Holliday saw that the bottom and all four sides were lined with carefully welded sheets of gold – a box within a box. Neatly etched into the gold were what looked like schematics for a series of strangely convoluted circuits – a wiring diagram or . . . 'What the hell is it?'

'I know it like the back of my hand,' said Rafi, awe still in his voice. 'Every archaeologist in the Middle East does, as well. I dug there as a student on my first field trip.'

Holliday suddenly saw it. Plans for a settlement of some sort. 'Why is it so important?'

'These are the plans for the settlement at Khirbet Qumran, the place where the Essenes wrote the Dead Sea Scrolls. The large drawing on the bottom is for the Scriptorium, the Essene library of their beliefs. There is clear evidence that in His early days Christ was converted to the Essene Creed and formulated his own teaching into theirs.'

There was a sudden commotion outside the palace and a small crowd began to form. A young man in a white tunic appeared, something cupped in his hand.

At first Holliday thought it was some strange insect the boy had found, but then the boy tipped the object into Fawcett's hands.

'What on earth is it?'

Holliday looked down at the object. It was about four inches long with roughly the same wingspan. The narrow body looked like some lightweight polymer, and the wings looked as though they were made of black, ultrathin sheets of mica. The creature's single tiny eye was obviously a camera.

'It's an X-Drifter. They're microsurveillance drones powered by sunlight and dropped in swarms from a larger unmanned vehicle like a Predator. Originally it was part of British Aerospace's WASP division, Winged Aerial Surveillance Program. It was then taken over by the Pallas Group, which in turn is owned by my old enemy Kate Sinclair. They've been looking for us – now it seems they've found us.'

James Calthrop reached the Gare de Bercy a full two hours before his train left for Rome. He'd booked both a private compartment and a single coach seat on the Artesia night train. The train left at seven p.m., traveling through Dijon, Parma, Bologna and Florence before arriving in Rome at eight the following morning. The thirteen-hour trip was a rattrap for whatever cutout ghost assassin Constantine sent, but after twenty-five years assassinating people for a living, Calthrop knew most of the ways of the art, including being prey as well as predator.

Bercy was a relatively new passenger station, built in the Seventies to replace the existing freight station. The terminal was only three floors high, and sitting in the waiting room it was possible to see everyone coming into the station or leaving it.

Calthrop spotted his quarry less than twenty minutes before the train left. The man was in his fifties or early sixties, round-faced, wearing wire-framed spectacles and an Ivy League cap used by a number of European men to hide their baldness. He wore a long, slightly rumpled brown cloth raincoat, scuffed brown shoes and carried an old-fashioned single-flap dispatch case under his arm.

The man was utterly nondescript, the picture of a low-level bureaucrat with a timeless, weary look of faint worry on his face. His wife would be fat, his children would whine and he would have few, if any, friends. Most people wouldn't give him a second glance.

Calthrop, of course, was no ordinary person. The man whose job it was to fade into the background for all his brownness and wallflower appearance was perhaps just a little too perfect, the raincoat artfully rumpled to show his lack of care about his own appearance coupled with a clear vanity in the wearing of the tweedy little cap. Which meant that the cap was really worn to cover a recognizable baldness or even more likely a full head of hair, perhaps gray or even white. The man's cheeks were perfectly shaven, even under the jaw, and the brown shoes were expensive brogues, either English or American and far too new to be that scuffed without the appropriate wearing down of the heels. He was a picture painted to look invisible, but the very artfulness of the image gave him away.

His weapon of choice would not be a gun; he traveled too much for that. It would be a knife hidden to look like something else or even more likely a garrote masquerading as an extra pair of shoelaces for the nicely scuffed shoes he wore. He was prepared for either – the advantage of having been a Boy Scout and perhaps one even Lord Baden-Powell would have approved of, considering the origins of his own expertise.

All of this went through Calthrop's mind in under a minute, watching as the man shuffled across the terminal floor to the ticket wicket. Calthrop kept watching as the man purchased his ticket and headed for the platform. He was traveling on the Artesia. Calthrop gave the man in the Ivy League cap a little head start, then followed the man sent to kill him on to the train.

*

Yachay, shaman and chief of the river people, had been running through the forest for many days now. He had no real idea of the time or distance he'd traveled, following only the whispering of his gods and the directions given to him through the *xhenhet*. He kept a wadded paste combined with bark from the magnolia in the side of his cheek, spitting it out and replacing it with another lump from the small leather bag tied around his waist.

They had already found the packs of explosives in the cache where his friend from the Mountain of the Gods had left them, and now the fifty warriors strung out behind him each carried twenty-five kilograms of the magic death-bringer and killer of monsters – a little more than two tons of plasticized pentaerythritol tetranitrate, perhaps the most violent plastic explosive in the world and the essential ingredient in its better known relative, Semtex.

Two tons of the pentaerythritol tetranitrate detonated with a small length of Primacord would be more than enough to rip the huge dam apart and send the waters that were the life of the river people back on its natural course. Detonation was simple since the detonation of a single molded handful of the Silly Putty substance would automatically detonate all the packs placed around it.

Yachay suddenly stopped, one hand lifted to halt the men behind them. He had lived his life in the forest and by the river and knew its sounds and smells, its creatures and the very air in the treetops above his head as though it were his own heart beating in his chest and his own lungs breathing. He could not say what it was or where it came from, but there was something wrong. A vibration, a sound out of the symphony of the forest and rippling of the river. A thought stirring and saying only one thing. Run! Run now!

22

The Canadair firebombers, tail identification spray-painted out, came in low, following the heat-signal directions given to them by the Super Tucanos flying surveillance in front of the slower-moving Canadairs.

It was almost dusk as the six aircraft dropped down even lower to two hundred feet, where they dropped the thick streams of jellied gasoline from the specially involved nozzles in their tanks, raining the napalm mixture down on the jungle below.

With the viscous mixture dripping from the forest canopy, two following Super Tucanos fired a total of eight M156 white phosphorous rockets into the center of the napalm path below and then immediately peeled away over the remains of the Itaqui River Basin, their pilots knowing the effect the rockets would have.

As the trigger charges in the rockets' proximity fuses struck, the rockets' white-hot explosions served as igniter for the napalm torrent that had followed only moments before. On the ground the aerated gasoline exploded, sucking the oxygen out of the air more effectively than any vacuum pump, immediately creating a mini-Dresden, a firestorm that blossomed out of nowhere, destroying, charring and liquefying everything in its path.

Had the two following Tucanos not peeled away as quickly as they did, the empty hole in the atmosphere would have sucked them down like the turbulence caused by the sinking of the *Titanic*. Even at that speed the aircraft barely escaped being engulfed by the huge, towering billow of fire that hurled itself up out of the rainforest like a biblical warning from God.

Yachay had presciently felt the aircraft coming to him with their cargoes of death at least a minute before the first aircraft arrived and almost two minutes before the napalm was ignited. He had acted on the inner voices of his gods, at once calling out a warning as he turned away from the edge of the jungle close to the drying riverbed, racing deeper into the forest where his only protection lay.

It was not to be. The rolling pressure wave struck him in the back like a hammer, throwing him to the forest floor, and then the gigantic blowback from the fireball sucked into the center of the white-hot maelstrom. In his last split second of consciousness as his lungs swallowed fire, Yachay knew that there were no gods and never had been and with that terrible sadness filling him he happily gave himself to the dark, unable to scream his fury as his lungs shriveled to cinders and his body vaporized.

It had been a coordinated attack, the firebombing coming at the same time as the White Star C130 Hercules dropped its seventy-man stick of paratroopers and two White Star M126 helicopters each landed a contingent of highly trained commandos on the summit of the mountain. At the mountain's base five of the paratroopers from the Hercules dropped with pinpoint accuracy at the mouth of the huge cavern holding the Devil's Throat and immediately began firing on Francisco Garibaldi and the already gagged Tanaki, who had previously been captured by Garibaldi. Three of the commandos took up their stations around the Devil's Throat and waited for further orders while the other two carried the bodies into the jungle and buried them in shallow graves before decomposition set in.

'We must leave immediately,' said a frightened-looking Hiram. The paratroopers were dropping into the canyon by the dozen.

'Hold on,' said Holliday, watching as the paratroopers descended. They were using rectangular 'ram air' canopies, the same guided system the U.S. Skydiving Team used, picking their spots in small clearings on the canyon floor. 'We have to think this through. Is there any place the box can be hidden where these guys won't find it? We can't take it with us. It's far too heavy.'

'Yes.' Hiram nodded, pulling himself together. He clapped his hands and the bearers reappeared. He gave them a quick order and they took the ossuary out of the main chamber on its litter.

'We must leave now. We're running out of time.'

'I heard choppers. The summit is certain to be crawling with men. Is there any other way we can leave without climbing the stairs?'

'There is a hidden way,' said Fawcett.

'Take us to it.'

Led by Fawcett and Hiram, both carrying fuming wick lamps, Holliday, Peggy, Eddie and Rafi maneuvered their way through a convoluted labyrinth of tunnels and small caves until they finally reached a large narrow cavern with a narrow stream running down its center.

There were half a dozen men already waiting. Instead of the tunics Holliday was used to seeing the people in, these men were dressed in dungarees and ragged shirts, their feet encased in rubber tire sandals. Strapped to their backs were large wicker baskets.

'Enough supplies to take you to the Essequibo River and then upriver to Bartica.' Hiram took a step back and bowed deeply. 'Good luck,' he said. 'May all the gods be with you and protect you on your journey.'

'You're not coming?' Holliday asked.

'I cannot leave my people.'

'They will kill you, my friend,' said Eddie. 'These are hard people.'

'Then I will die,' said Hiram, shrugging. 'That is my fate. Now go.'

With Fawcett leading the way, the others followed him along the path of the stream to a small exit covered by drooping fire vine. Parting the vine, they ducked out through the opening into the dusky evening light.

A few yards outside the opening, a striking man with snow-white hair stood calmly, backed by an eight-man squad. The white-haired man was dressed in paratrooper camo, puttees wrapped over the high tops of his jump boots. He had a white star on one breast pocket and a wide silver stripe on the other.

'Dr Fawcett, Colonel Holliday, I presume?' He turned to his squad and nodded. Six members of the squad lifted their modified Stokes MK22 handguns, aimed and then fired at almost point-blank range.

James Calthrop waited until they reached the railway terminal in Parma for a ten-minute stop to switch crews. He stepped out on to the platform for a cigarette and looked up and down the sleeping car from the outside. All the curtains were fully drawn and there was no light to be seen anywhere. A hundred-euro bribe to the trainman had purchased him the compartment number of the man he'd seen at Bercy Station, and beyond that Calthrop was already well prepared.

The man would not likely make his attack until after Florence, the last stop before reaching Rome. That way there would be the least chance of discovery, and before the body was found the killer would have more than enough time to disappear into the throngs of people at the busiest railway terminal in Italy.

The warning horn sounded, the trainman at the head end blew his whistle and Calthrop tossed down the butt of his cigarette and stepped back on the train, the automatic door swishing shut. There was a sudden surge of motion, and they moved smoothly out of the station and into the suburban darkness of Bologna.

Calthrop moved without hesitation. He dipped his hand into his pocket briefly, slipped on a pair of leather gloves and then walked down the barely lit corridor and rapped quietly on his quarry's door.

'*Scusa, signor . . .*'

The response was too quick and alert. The killer was wide-awake. '*Chi è?*'

'*Il controllore, signor.*'

'Un momento.'

Calthrop drew the silenced Berretta Tomcat from its sling under his arm and waited for the click of the killer's latch being opened. When it came he put his left shoulder against the door and heaved forward, expecting the resistant body of the killer. Instead there was nothing and he went tumbling into the compartment, barely able to bring his hand up to his neck before the loop of steel wire was dropped around it.

The wire, a diamond-dust bead reamer and cutter, bit through the glove but didn't fare so well when it struck the leather bondage collar under Calthrop's shirt – purchased the previous day at La Passage du Désir on Rue St Martin.

There was a split second of hesitation at the unexpected resistance to the nearly razor-sharp device, and the man strained harder. To exert that kind of force meant the killer's head was almost certainly tilted back, and aiming blindly, Calthrop lifted the Tomcat and fired. The small .22-caliber round struck the man under the chin, went through the tongue and palate and then entered the skull, slicing up into the brain and ricocheting several times until it lodged somewhere in the chewed-up remains of the corpus callosum. The killer was a corpse before he knew he'd taken his last breath. There was almost no blood.

Calthrop, on the other hand, was bleeding profusely.

The killer dropped to the floor and Calthrop staggered toward the little bathroom cubicle. He dropped down on to the toilet, grabbed one of the thin towels off the rack, then gently peeled off his glove. The bead reamer had cut through the leather and deeply into the flesh of his index and middle fingers. Feeling a little faint, he wrapped the towel around his hand tightly, then lifted the bound hand and stuffed it into the sling that held the Tomcat holster, keeping it raised. He leaned back and closed his eyes, willing the light-headed feeling to fade away. He wasn't finished yet and he had to think clearly.

Calthrop gave himself ten minutes, then stood, left the cubicle and eased himself around the dead body. If things had gone as he'd hoped they would, he would have put the killer into his bunk and pulled the blankets over him. Like Calthrop, the man had purchased a through ticket to Rome and no one would check his compartment until they arrived at their final destination. As it was, that option was impossible now, so he simply stepped over the body, peeked out into the corridor to make sure the way was clear and returned to his own compartment, locking the door behind him.

Once inside, he took down his overnight bag, pulled out a spare shirt and using the scissors on his Swiss Army knife, he sliced into the fabric, eventually cutting half a dozen long strips. That done, he took the strips to the bathroom, turned on the tap over the sink and then gingerly unbound the towel around his hand. The wounds weren't as bad as he'd thought, but they definitely needed attention. He dropped the bloody towel into the sink, then used three of the strips from his shirt to bind the two fingers tightly together and finally wound the rest of the strips around his entire hand. He waited for a few moments, but no blood seeped through. He looked into the mirror over the sink, dabbed away a small blob of some sort of human tissue on his cheek and then went back into the compartment. He tore the plastic refuse bag off the wall beside the toilet, dropped the bloody towel as well as the bondage collar and the ruined shirt into it, then stuffed it into his overnight bag. He sat down on the edge of his bunk and waited. At seven sixteen the train arrived at the Florence terminal. Calthrop picked up the overnight bag with his good hand, left his compartment and stepped off the train a few moments later, disappearing into the anonymous crowd on the platform.

Constantine sat in one of the worn upholstered chairs in the apartment reading that day's edition of *La Repubblica*. It was late, past twelve now, and the Paris–Rome train arrived just after nine. His breakfast of a cannoli and coffee was nothing but crumbs and dregs in his cup on the small table to his right. He wasn't surprised; in fact, he'd been expecting something like this.

There was a triple rap on the door of the apartment. 'Enter.'

Calthrop stepped into the front room. He looked tired but alert. His left hand was neatly wrapped in surgical bandage.

'Hurt?' Constantine asked, his voice mild.

'A little,' said Calthrop. 'You don't seem surprised to see me.'

'I'm not, particularly,' said Constantine, lowering the newspaper.

'You sent someone to kill me.'

'You knew too much.'

'He failed,' said Calthrop, taking the Tomcat out from under his jacket.

'One of you had to,' said Constantine. 'It was simply a matter of which of you it was going to be.'

'Now I'm going to kill you,' said Calthrop.

Constantine fired the Tanfoglio T95 from underneath the newspaper, striking Calthrop twice in the chest and once in the abdomen.

'Not if I kill you first,' said Constantine to the dead man.

23

Holliday came to, feeling as if someone were running a clattering old wringer washer inside his skull. For a long time he kept his eyes closed, pretty sure that opening them wasn't going to make the wringer washer stop any faster.

He lay there, letting things come back slowly. The last thing he remembered clearly was the squad of soldiers standing in front of them and the white-haired old pro with the silver stripe on his camo BDUs.

He remembered that the camo was old-fashioned Vietnam-era Tiger Stripe pattern, which the U.S. Army hadn't used in forty years. Ergo, these guys weren't regulars.

He had a vague recollection of a white star on the BDUs, and then he had it. He'd read somewhere that Black Hawk Security, Kate Sinclair's organization through the Pallas Group, had recently changed its name to White Star. His heart sank. Kate Sinclair again, still searching for the relic she thought would mitigate all the foul deeds done to get it. The personification of the ends justifying the means even though it meant ruining lives that got in her way.

He remembered the men firing from only a few yards away. He must have been hit, but all he felt was a deep bruiselike sensation on the right side of his ribs. After that there was nothing but a jumbled blur. He let a little more time pass, breathing slowly and deeply, taking in as much oxygen as he could. He wasn't dead, that was clear enough, but he'd almost certainly been drugged – that was the washing machine doing the fandango in his skull.

The blur of fractured memory began to resolve itself. Rotors. He listened to the memory: the distinct humming, thundering blender sounds of a big Jolly Green Giant like the ones they'd used for spec-ops in Vietnam. Twenty-five troops in full gear with a range of seven hundred miles if you stuck an extra tank somewhere. More than enough to take them to a base on the Atlantic Coast, probably Guyana.

After that, nothing, or next to nothing. Maybe the sound of a big diesel engine lumbering to life, and definitely a reek of shrimp or clams or some sort of crustacean. Then a quick sharp pain and blackness again.

A boat then, probably a trawler of some kind. But how long had he been out and where was he now? He sniffed; his own clothes smelled like rotting fish, but the air was dry and stale.

There was no sense that he was close to the ocean, or at least not close enough to smell it in the air. On a guess he was somewhere that hadn't been used for a very long time.

The wringer washer was fading now, so he opened his eyes slowly. They were gummy with a crust of old protein on the eyelids. He'd been out for a few days at the very least. His eyes squinted open. No natural light, just a low-watt bulb behind a wire cage in the ceiling and nothing else.

He pulled himself into a sitting position and took stock of his surroundings. He was on an old-fashioned cot that could very well have been army issue at one time.

There was an upended wooden box beside him with a PowerBar and a small bottle of Crystal Springs water. He suddenly realized how hungry and thirsty he was. He was no fool, though; he ate half the bar and drank half the water. Who knew when food or drink was going to come round again?

The room came into focus as he chewed on the protein bar. Four bare walls of some kind of flimsy pressboard painted pale green, the ceiling made of old acoustic tiles stained by leaks and who knew how many cigarettes turning the squares a sick-looking nicotine shade. The floor was concrete covered with some kind of gray paint. The door was plain wood fitted with what appeared to be a brand-new Schlage lock.

There was a calendar thumbtacked to the wall.

June 1956 with a day circled in faded ink and a note: 400 LB. FF DARBY/FOB; KNOX. The top of the calendar had a picture of an old C47 with the name Tarpon Air Cargo on the fuselage and a red leaping tarpon on a deep blue background painted on the tail. At the bottom of the photograph was an address: JOSEPH BOSARGE FIELD BAYOU LA BATRE ALABAMA — WE GET IT WHERE YOU WANT WHEN YOU WANT.

It was starting to make sense. No one would think twice about a trawler full of shrimp coming into an Alabama shrimp town, and he was willing to bet Joseph Bosarge Field hadn't been used in decades. In all likelihood they were probably being kept here until they'd been questioned and/or a plane came in to take them wherever they were supposed to go.

The year before, he'd read a Lee Child thriller about people being dropped from helicopters high over the Nevada desert. He knew from personal experience what that was like.

He'd seen men from one of the Ranger Long Range Reconnaissance Patrols, or LRRPS, dropping suspected Vietcong spies from choppers up a thousand feet or so as an incentive for their colleagues to talk. Grisly, but effective. Taking a flight out into the gulf and dropping him and the others would be just as useful.

First question — was he alone or were the others

nearby? Holliday looked carefully at the walls and the ceiling, paying special attention to the industrial light fixture. He ran his hands across the walls at eye level and lower and examined the four corners.

The room didn't appear to be bugged and there was no telltale fuzzing of the texture of the walls where there might be a fiber-optic camera embedded. He went to the wall on his left and banged it hard with his fist. He waited, listening, but there was no response.

He repeated the process on the left wall. This time he got an answer. It was in Morse code: dash, dot, dot – Delta – dash, dash, dash – Oscar – dash, dot, dash, dot – Charlie – dash, dash, dot, dot – Interrogative. 'Doc?'

Holliday rapped back a quick double tap – Affirmative. He stepped back. All Israelis did compulsory military service, but was Rafi old enough to have learned the old-fashioned code? On the other hand, Eddie almost certainly had. Holliday had a quick conversation through the wall.

'Eddie?'

'Yes.'

'The others?'

'Here. Next to me.'

'Safe?

'All good, I think. Other rooms. Where we are?'

Holliday smiled. Even in Morse the Cuban could

get his grammar screwed up. Or was it someone pretending to be Eddie? A shill put in to get information?

'Your brother's name?'

'Domingo. Why you ask?'

Holliday relaxed. 'Checking.'

A rapid dot-dot-dot-dash-dot for 'Understood.'

'How get out?'

'Walls flimsy. Door flimsy, too.'

'Count ten and go.'

'Affirmative.'

At five the door opened of its own accord and a grunt in White Star camo gear stepped into the room. No more tranquilizer guns. This one was holding a Mossberg 500 combat shotgun. There was a SIG Sauer P220 in an open holster on his hip. 'Outside,' he said. 'Slowly.'

Holliday nodded once and did as he was told.

24

Holliday stepped out of the little room, the White Star man with the shotgun backing up, the big Mossberg aimed at his belly. Holliday found himself in an old-fashioned corrugated Quonset hut. The rusty metal curved above his head, and the far end had a pair of big sliding doors, both of which were open, flooding the entire space with natural light. Beyond the doors Holliday could see the front end of a white panel truck, and out on the cracked tarmac of a runway he saw an old C47 with its cargo door open. The livery was a two-tone blue-and-white with the name OPELOUSAS AIR TRANSPORT along the fuselage. Beyond that was a line of screening trees.

Eddie, Peggy and Rafi appeared, Peggy and Rafi looking a bit dazed, Eddie with that hard look on his face that meant he was barely controlling his anger. There was no sign of Harrison Fawcett.

Four folding wooden chairs were set out on the concrete. The chairs looked as old as the calendar on the wall of Holliday's room. The guards gestured toward the chairs and they sat down.

'Everyone okay?' Holliday asked.

'We're okay,' said Rafi.

'Mama pinga,' Eddie said, sneering.

'Not good.'

'No good at all – for them.'

'Not yet,' answered Holliday.

Eddie began to hum his old campfire song; never a good sign. Very much like the grumbling sound the earth makes before a volcano is about to erupt.

'Where's Fawcett?' Holliday asked.

'I never saw him after we came out of the cave. He just seemed to vanish,' answered Rafi.

'Shut the fuck up!' one of the guards barked. They all shut up. All except Eddie, who kept on humming. A couple of minutes later a Lincoln Town Car swept in through the open doors of the Quonset hut. A man got out of the backseat. He was wearing an expensive suit, expensive shoes and had the self-assured stance of a patrician background. A pair of neon red half-frame bifocals were perched on the end of his nose.

'Charlie Peace,' Holliday said. 'I haven't seen you since you ran that crappy little airline for us in Afghanistan. I seem to remember punching your lights out after one of your drunken jerk-off pilots killed six of my men by flying into a mountain.'

'Times change, Colonel. I'm at the top of the heap now, and you're the one down in the trenches.'

'I guess we'll have to wait until we see who the last man standing is, Charlie.'

'I guess we will,' said Charles Peace, CEO of the Pallas Group and through them the owner of the largest private army in the world.

'I notice Fawcett's missing,' said Holliday, keeping his eyes on Peace. One of the guards brought the tall, dark-haired man a chair. He sat down, pulled a silver cigarette case out of the pocket of his suit and lit up, using what looked like a vintage Zippo with a U.S. Marine Corps seal.

'You meet some *Semper Fi* guy in a bar somewhere and he sees that, you'll be in trouble,' warned Holliday.

'I rarely meet people in bars,' said Peace.

'What about Fawcett?'

'We discovered Mr Fawcett quite some time ago,' Peace answered. 'Like any man, he had his price. He's been taking samples for us to examine. We've built a whole little corporation in Switzerland around his exotic little plants.' Peace crossed his legs, meticu lously lifting the razor crease on his trousers. 'That's beside the point, of course. What I really want to know about is the disposition of the relic.'

Holliday laughed, his voice ringing in the old air- plane hangar. 'What is it with you people and relics?' He shook his head. 'You really think some Holy Grail or Shroud of Turin or the Ark of the Covenant is going to give you supreme power?

'Hitler thought that and he was nuts. I just don't get it. I've been ducking you people for years because you think I've got a direct line to Relics-R-Us? The Indiana Jones movies are great stories, but this is the real world we're in, Charlie. You of all people should know that.

'You're a jacked-up mercenary in a sharp suit. You deal in reality every day. You really believe that these things have some kind of power you can use like some sort of cosmic battery? If you do you're as crazy as Adolf. Kate Sinclair might be that much of a loony, Charlie, but not you.'

'Are you finished?' Peace asked.

'For the moment,' answered Holliday.

'Aliens,' said Peace.

'Pardon?'

'I have very little time for any of this, Colonel, but I'll give you one or two examples, aliens being the first one. What do you think of the work of Erich von Däniken?'

'Another loser.'

'A loser who made millions of dollars, sold untold copies of his books in a hundred languages, spawned a television industry and put a rocket up the ass of the science fiction movie genre. In all, several billion dollars generated out of some odd xenophobia. You don't call that power?'

'The second example?'

'Lourdes, St Jude, the Basilica in Montreal, Jesus tacos, weeping Mary statues, Joan of Arc, Bethlehem, Dan Brown books, Satanist Masons, black helicopters. Faith, Colonel Holliday. It can move mountains, start wars, kill millions of people. And it's intangible and invisible. It's not the relic, Colonel. It's the idea of the relic. It's the idea of it that has the power.

'There are two point eight billion Christians in the world. A hundred and fifty million Americans believe God created the universe in seven days. That's half the population of the country, Colonel, and they all believe in the relic.

'You could probably elect a president if you could get a photo op of him with his hand on it. If the Catholic Church had it – and let me assure you, they want it very badly – it could give them back all the power and credibility they've steadily been losing for the last two thousand years. Knowledge is power, Colonel Holliday, and the relic is the ultimate knowledge. God made manifest on the earth.'

'Quite a speech, Charlie, but what does it have to do with me?'

'The relic was in Fawcett's idea of Jurassic Park. His father saw it almost a hundred years ago. It's not in Jurassic Park now.'

'How do you know that?'

'We looked.' Peace dropped his cigarette and

ground it out with the sole of his expensive-looking shoe. 'So where is it?'

'I have no idea.'

'Of course you do, Colonel. That Hiram character showed it to you.'

'Who told you that, Fawcett?'

'That's right.'

'And you believe him.'

'Certainly. More than I believe you.'

'What about Hiram? Did you speak to him?'

'Never found him. Fawcett knew a lot of places to look, but if the old man existed in the first place, he must have slipped away.'

'Charlie,' chided Holliday, 'I thought you were a big-time executive now. You can't put those two facts together? The relic and the man whose entire family going back to the beginning was charged with protecting it have both disappeared?'

Peace's expression darkened. He turned to one of the guards. 'Duct-tape all of them, hands behind their backs, feet as well. Load them on to the plane when it comes and when you get far enough out over the gulf, toss them through the cargo hatch and keep on tossing until one of them talks. Keep the colonel for last; let him watch his friends go screaming into eternity. Maybe then he'll feel more like talking. Call me when he does. I'm going into town for some crab claws at Sidney's.'

*

William Copeland Black, late of MI5, recently seconded to 'Big Sister' MI6, sat in Pat Philpot's office at the National Center for Counter-terrorism in Tysons Corner in Virginia sipping a glass of Philpot's cheap Scotch and watching as the fat man across from him methodically wheezed and chewed his way through a Mighty Caesar Chicken Salad, a matched pair of Double Big Macs, a side of fries, a snack of twelve McNuggets and a large Oreo McFlurry with two caramel apple pies thrown into the McFlurry just for fun.

Black could almost feel the man's tortured heart crying out for mercy, and the overflowing ashtray on the man's desk didn't say much for the state of his lungs. Black remembered the scene in Monty Python's *The Meaning of Life* when Mr Creosote literally exploded from gorging at a restaurant.

Philpot paused in his suicidal grazing of the food-like objects spread across his desk, lit a Marlboro and leaned back in his frighteningly straining office chair. 'Where are we on all this crap?' Philpot jerked a thumb over his shoulder at the complicated connective 'nodes' chart on the whiteboard behind him.

'Murky at best,' answered Black. 'There are links between the Vatican Bank, White Horse Resources and all the rest of Lord Grayle's evil empire, your fellow Peace's Pallas Group, the disappearance of Percy Fawcett eighty or ninety years ago and various and sundry assassinations, most of them in Italy but one in Switzerland. Grayle's involvement with White Glove or the Masons or whatever secret society is the big thing these days that seems to provide some connective tissue, as well, much of it through Kate Sinclair. All very obscure.'

'You see the locus of all of this? The spider at the center of the web, even though he doesn't know it?' Philpot said, inhaling deeply.

'Lieutenant Colonel John Holliday,' responded Black, sighing. 'We've run across him more than once,' he said. 'His uncle Henry Granger worked with us as far back as World War Two, along with a man named Sir Derek Carr-Harris.'

'We've had a relationship with him since Iraq – the first one. The Vatican doesn't like him, Kate Sinclair blames him for the suicides of both her son and her daughter and the company's had trouble with him from one end of the world to the other.'

'On the other hand, he saved your bacon and mine during that Cuba fiasco.'

Philpot finished his cigarette and picked up a McNugget, dipping it into three separate sauces and popping it into his mouth before it dripped on his tie.

'I think we've got to pull him off the game board,' said Philpot, chewing.

'Neutralize him?'

'I'm afraid so. Some rigorous interrogation first, but in the end he needs to go. So does his friend the Cuban. I don't know how much he's told his cousin Miss Blackstock and her husband, but they'll have to go, as well.'

'May I ask why?'

'Because he knows far more than is good for him and far more than both your government and mine think is good for them.

'Look at the chart. He's central to all of it. We're talking about what game designers call the "Overworld." Governments don't run the world – these people and organizations do. Most people aren't even aware of it. It's the big machine, Mr Black, and Colonel Holliday keeps on putting a monkey wrench through the gears. He just won't leave the status quo alone, I'm afraid. It's not in Doc's nature, I suppose, which is why he really does have to go.'

It was Eddie who made the first move. A few moments after Peace drove off in his limo, a third guard appeared carrying a brown paper bag in his hand. He pulled out a roll of duct tape and stepped forward, putting his hand on Eddie's shoulder.

'*Me cago en tu madre, cabrón!*' Eddie lurched upward, hammering his shoulder into the guard's solar plexus, then slipped on the oily floor and fell back, knocking Holliday out of his chair. He struggled to get up, but one of the other guards stepped forward and clubbed Eddie with the butt of his riot gun.

They were taped hand and foot with a strip across their mouths for good measure, and then one by one they were loaded on to the plane waiting outside. One of the guards remained behind to wait for Peace to return, and the other two climbed on to the plane.

Holliday had been the first one dumped on to the ribbed metal floor of the old transport, and he could see that there was only one man in the cockpit. After five minutes of going through his procedures, the twin engines guttered into asthmatic life, then leveled off and the pilot started the old girl moving.

Holliday carefully opened his clenched fist and checked the small object Eddie had forced into his hand during his dramatic little tirade in the old hangar. It was about four inches long, thin and extremely sharp for the first inch of its length. At a guess Eddie had found a loose spring in the iron bed in his little room and worked it loose. Presumably he was carrying a piece of the spring, as well.

Holliday began to work with it, twisting the piece of metal around in his hand and poking, then sawing at the tape.

It took more than twenty minutes, but he finally managed to cut through the tape. He checked the disposition of the guards. They were both sitting on the old jump seats directly across from him, Mossbergs between their legs, chatting with the pilot, completely ignoring their bound and gagged passengers.

That was about to change.

Holliday suddenly lifted his knees, dug in his heels and tried to lift his shoulders into a sitting position against the jump seats on the opposite side of the aircraft.

The guard directly in front of him growled and stood up, the Mossberg raised to clout him as he'd done to Eddie in the hangar. As he stepped forward, Eddie swung his legs around, sweeping the guard off his feet. The Mossberg went flying and the guard fell directly on top of Holliday, who pulled his hands out from under him.

He used one hand to grab the throat of the guard's camo BDUs and bring him down even harder while the hand holding the piece of steel drove up and buried itself in the guard's throat.

As blood gurgled and spat from the guard's neck, Eddie found the holster on his hip, grabbed the SIG Sauer and planted three rounds in the second guard – two to the chest and one to the head. The whole thing took less than fifteen seconds. Holliday tore the tape away from his mouth.

'Shit!' Holliday yelled. 'The pilot!' The man from the cockpit pushed his way into the cargo bay, some sort of weapon in his hand. Eddie reacted instinctively, emptying the last five rounds from the SIG into the man, blowing back toward the cockpit. The plane flew on without a twitch, brainlessly taking them farther and farther out into the Gulf of Mexico. Somewhere during the DC3's long life, Holliday guessed an autopilot had been installed.

Holliday and Eddie freed Peggy and Rafi, then opened one of the 'barn doors' of the cargo hatch and tossed the bodies of the two guards and the pilot out into the clear, bright blue of the afternoon sky. Five thousand feet straight down into the dark waters of the gulf. They wrestled the door closed and walked back toward the front of the plane.

'I have a question,' said Peggy.

'Shoot,' said Holliday.

'Does anyone know how to fly this crate?'

Arturo Bonnifacio, Cardinal Ruffino, secretary of state for the Holy See, met with his Secret Service director and longtime lover, Vittorio Monti, in the back room at Dino and Tony's. The cardinal was enjoying a plate of deep-fried artichoke leaves called *carciofi alla giudia* and a glass of Epomeo Colli del Sangro. Monti sipped an espresso.

The cardinal ate one of the crunchy, nutty leaves, then took a sip of wine. 'What is our present status?'

'Calthrop is dead, so is DiMarco, the cutout and

Garibaldi, or at least he hasn't sent us his scheduled contact.'

'Calthrop, you're sure?'

'I did it myself. Either he or DiMarco was going to come through the door of the safe house. It was Calthrop, which meant that DiMarco was dead.'

'None of this will come back to us, I hope.'

'Of course not. They both knew me only as Constantine. The landlord rents to a man named Francesco Landini. We have our own in-house cleaners. The apartment will be spotless by now.'

'Holliday and his people?'

'Holliday's chip is still working. Apparently he is in some godforsaken place called Bayou La Batre in the state of Alabama.'

'At last glimpse he was in northern Brazil seeking out the relic. Why would he be in such a place?'

'I would say from the evidence that Grayle or another of your brother's friends has him.'

'What do you suggest we do?'

'For the time being, nothing. If the relic exists we'll hear about it. My sense is that Holliday is being interrogated. If the interrogation is successful, he will almost certainly be disposed of. Let the others involved in this paperchase do the work for us.'

'We cannot let Grayle's people have it,' Cardinal Ruffino said emphatically. 'It is too much power. It would tip the scales at a time when such a thing could virtually destroy us. We are already on the brink of insolvency.' Ruffino shook his head. 'My own brother,' he whispered. 'How could he?'

'Your brother is a pawn, a tailor with delusions of grandeur. What he does he does to hurt you.'

'Why?'

'Because he is weak. And because he is envious of you. You have achieved greatness, and perhaps even more awaits you. He is nothing and never will be.'

'You are a harsh man, Vittorio.'

'It is a harsh world, Arturo.'

25

'Eddie trained in the Cuban Air Force,' said Holliday. He turned to his friend.

'Helicopters,' said Eddie. 'Not in tractors like this.'

'You must have had some training on fixed-wing aircraft. You flew that thing we stole in Russia.'

'That thing was an Antonov-2, a single-engine biplane that a good horse could outrun. It is used for crop-dusting. It also happens to be the only fixed-wing I ever trained on, amigo.'

'Oh, crap,' Peggy said. 'We've got fifty miles of water underneath us and no Sully Sullenberger to drive the bus.'

'*Qué?*' Eddie said.

'Forget it,' answered Peggy.

'Look,' said Rafi. 'Eddie's the only one who's had any flying training at all. We can either sit here flying toward the Yucatán until we run out of gas or Eddie can strap into the pilot's thing and try to get us back on the ground.'

'Rafi's right,' said Holliday. 'We really don't have any other way to go.'

'You will be my copilot, *compañero*?'

'Sure,' said Holliday.

'Is there anything we can do?' Peggy asked.

'Pray, Senora Peggy. Pray very hard.'

Eddie slipped into the pilot's bucket seat, touching nothing, his eyes scanning the controls to his right, the instrument panel in front of the yoke and the overhead electronics panel. 'There is no automatic pilot here,' said Eddie. 'This airplane is very Cuban. A pair of engines and some wings.'

'The plane was flying that steadily all by itself?' Holliday said.

'It would seem that way, my friend,' the Cuban answered. 'Rudder pedals, ailerons, throttles, pitch. Maybe Senora Peggy was right. This really is a *guagua*.'

'Gwah-gwah?' Holliday asked.

'Bus,' answered Eddie, still studying the controls. He spent a few more moments figuring out the basic layout and then nodded. 'First we must turn the bus around.'

Holliday had his eye on the simple float compass mounted dead center on top of the dashboard or whatever you called it on an airplane. They had been flying almost due southeast into an almost black horizon heavy with storm clouds.

'Left rudder, turn left,' Eddie muttered. He eased his foot down on the left pedal and gently gripped the yoke and turned it in the same direction. Slowly but surely the lumbering DC3 began to turn. There was a sudden, unpleasant coughing sound.

'What's that?' Holliday asked. Eddie toggled a switch on a floor plate at the foot of the console, and there was a definite surge of power.

'Reserve tanks,' explained Eddie.

Holliday's eyes were glued to the float compass. As slowly as Eddie turned the aircraft around, the needle on the compass swung through a hundred and eighty degrees. After a long three minutes, the compass read north by northwest. 'That's it,' said Holliday quietly.

Eddie eased his foot off the pedal and turned the yoke back until there wasn't even a flutter on the compass needle.

'Now what?' Holliday said.

'We must lose altitude and much speed before we attempt to reach the ground.'

Holliday checked the instrument panel in front of him. According to the gauges and dials, they were flying at just under two hundred miles per hour at eight thousand feet. He'd flown at thirty-eight thousand feet in a hundred passenger jets, but sitting here a mile and a half in the air seemed much higher.

They flew on for another half an hour, Eddie checking out the feel of the plane with delicate movements of the yoke. Holliday kept his mouth shut, his eyes on the compass course and occasionally checked over his shoulder at the blackening sky behind them. By his estimation they had less than thirty minutes to get the old bird on to the ground before the gathering tropical storm rolled over them and tore her wings off like a fly caught in a swirling toilet bowl.

The land ahead of them grew into a broad, thick line that slowly began to fill the bottom of the windscreen. 'Time to go down, amigo,' said Eddie. He eased back the throttle on both of the big engines, adjusted the flaps and nudged the yoke forward smoothly.

The aircraft's nose came down and she went into a smooth, shallow descent. Holliday turned his attention to the altimeter, eyes fixed on the dial as it spun downward, going through hundreds of feet like the second hand on a wristwatch. Holliday checked over his shoulder again; the storm was frighteningly close.

'Big storm on our tail, Eddie. We don't get down soon, it's going to be bad.'

Eddie took a quick look over his shoulder. '*Coño!*'

Almost instantly there was a rattling sound from the rear of the aircraft that sounded as though they were being strafed by some monstrous machine gun in the clouds. The sound was deafening and suddenly it was coming from directly overhead as golfball-sized pieces of hail hammered at the cockpit roof and began shattering on the Plexiglas in front of them.

Holliday had spotted the wiper switch right under the compass and leaned forward in his seat, toggling it on. The wipers heaved into life, smearing and scattering the skin of slush forming on the glass, and

Eddie instinctively pushed the nose forward, changing their dive angle steeply and sending the engines into a screaming paroxysm as he simultaneously throttled back.

Below them the waters of the gulf, broken and whitecapped, filled the windscreen. The crackling of lightning exploded around them, and the entire aircraft shuddered and rattled as the hail turned to rain so heavy the wipers only gave the smallest shred of visibility for an eyeblink of time.

Holliday watched the altimeter and as it spun its way down to a thousand feet, Eddie hauled back on the yoke, desperately trying to pull them out of the careening dive into the yawning cavernous abyss of the ocean below. At eight hundred feet Holliday felt the nose begin to come up. At six he could see land dead ahead and at three they thundered over the beach and the shrimp boats at the docks of Bayou la Batre.

'*El tren de aterrizaje de mierda!*' Eddie screamed, his eyes widening as he throttled back. 'The landing gear – where is it?'

Eddie looked around frantically. Holliday followed suit. There was nothing on the panel in front of them and nothing that he could see on the throttle and pitch console between them. The altimeter showed two hundred feet and was still twisting down. Dead ahead Holliday could just make out the runway through the slashing rain that hurled itself at the windscreen. Outside, the wind was howling and it was all Eddie could do to hang on to the yoke of the aircraft as it pitched and heaved like a bull in a rodeo.

As he muttered curses under his breath, the Cuban's eyes flickered to the altimeter. Holliday looked. Fifty feet and still falling.

'Hold on!' Eddie yelled. He reached out, grabbed the throttles and pushed them up and into the Off position, then hauled back on the yoke, bringing the nose of the aircraft up. The engines stuttered and then died, the now lifeless triple-bladed propellers chewing on dead air. At the last second the limousine Charlie Peace had arrived in rose like a black ghost coming out of the torrential downpour, and then they hit, slewing and bellying in on the grass beside the runway, spinning slowly, parts on the fuselage tearing off as it twisted around.

The starboard-side wing hit the limousine first, the forty-six-foot-long metal blade hacking through the roof of the vehicle like a farmer's scythe harvesting wheat. The plane continued its twisting journey along the grass, the tail assembly swinging around to hit the limousine a second time just as Charles Peace was desperately trying to exit what was left of the vehicle, crushing him into a bloody red smear against the bright white lower half of the plane.

Finally, reaching the end of its long pirouette, the plane stood up on its nose a little, the two big engines tearing themselves to pieces as they chewed into the dark soil. At last the old DC3 came to a stop. For a moment there was only the endless roar of the rain and the ticking of the aircraft as it finally came to rest. Holliday realized he'd been holding his breath.

'*Bueno?*' Eddie said quietly.

'*Bueno.*' Holliday nodded.

'A vow,' said Eddie.

'Shoot,' said Holliday.

'Never again,' said Eddie.

'Agreed,' said Holliday, and both men began to laugh hysterically.

Peggy poked her head into the cockpit. 'Whenever you guys stop laughing at your man joke, we better think about getting out of here. I don't think they get a lot of plane crashes around here, and buzzing the town at fifty feet or whatever it was is sure to have attracted attention.'

'Yeah, and we just drove an airplane through the body of the man who owns the biggest private army in the world. That's probably going to get us on CNN.'

'So what do we do now?' Peggy asked.

'We go to Miami,' said Rafi quietly. 'I know someone there who can help us.'

*

William Copeland Black sat in the secure MI6 'Pod' in the U.K. Embassy complex just off Observatory Circle in Washington, D.C., just about the only place you could smoke without being chastised by one and all.

Besides having the smoker's lamp perpetually lit, the Pod was blanketed in every kind of electronic countermeasure available. It had a self-contained ventilation and sprinkler system and had been built as a building within a building, the single entrance and exit through six air-lock-style revolving doors, which required closed-circuit, electronic and biometric checks on the people trying to enter or leave.

By those who worked there, it was generally referred to by its nickname, the Womb. The Womb lay in perpetual semi darkness lit mostly by the dozens of computer screens and desk lamps used by its occupants. The only relatively normal room in the place was the glass-walled conference area. The glass was electric and could be changed from translucent to opaque at the touch of a switch.

There were three other people in the Womb with Black: the embassy's commercial attaché and head of MI6 in the United States, Sir Alistair Sim; George Givens, representing the Home Office; and Roger Thornhill, the Womb's senior tech analyst.

'Apparently it's open season on Holliday and his little entourage,' said Black. 'Our cousins want him "off the game board," as Philpot put it. The Vatican has tried at least twice that we know of, and Kate Sinclair's coven of witches and warlocks are hell-bent on boiling Holliday in oil.'

'I understand Lord Grayle has a part to play in all of this, as well,' replied Sir Alistair.

'For now he seems to have thrown in his lot with Sinclair and the Pallas Group, although I can't see that lasting for very long.'

'This can't really be about some silly Indiana Jones artifact, can it?' George Givens asked. Givens was a thin, short and balding man who looked perpetually anxious. Black knew the type: a middle bureaucrat in the cogs of government terrified of putting a foot wrong. The kind of man who grew geraniums in his garden and made decisions like walking through glue.

'Actually we've been connected with Holliday's family since the war,' said Sir Alistair. 'His uncle was one of us in the Forties.'

'He and a man named Carr-Harris,' said Black. 'I've read the file.'

'You really are quite well informed.' Sir Alistair smiled. 'Supposedly they were working for the joint Monuments, Fine Arts and Archives section of the British and United States armies, trying to recover looted art and artifacts. What they were actually doing is a different story altogether.'

'Do tell,' said Black.

'They were following a number of clues that pointed to the existence of a ledger or notebook that listed all the banks, bank accounts, real estate, gold bullion and other treasures accumulated by the Poor Fellow-Soldiers of Christ and of the Temple of Solomon – the Templars. They might have been soldiers of Christ at one time, but they certainly weren't poor.'

'Poppycock,' said Givens. 'Conspiracy nutters on the Interweb.'

The MI6 head of station gave the little man a long, hard look. 'Hardly that, Mr Givens. They were today's equivalent of the Stichting INGKA Foundation.'

'It's a Dutch charity that is just a little smaller than the Bill and Melinda Gates Foundation.'

'Never heard of them,' scoffed Givens.

'It owns IKEA among other things. We don't really know what it does with its thirty-six billion dollars every year, just like the pope and the king of France didn't know much about the Templars. A secretive bunch, I must say. But the king and the pope and our own dear Richard the Lionheart borrowed heavily from them. Think of a tax-free status for the greatest usurers and loan sharks the world has ever seen. Derek Carr-Harris and Holliday's uncle, Henry Granger, never found the ledger, but we think Holliday somehow did. And there are a great many dangerous people out there who would love to take it away from Holliday, or at least have a peek into its pages.'

'So what do we do with him?' Black asked.

'I suggest we go against the grain a little. Let's bring him in and question him. If he's uncooperative we can always throw him to the wolves again.' Sir Alistair turned to Thornhill, who was busily tapping away at the keyboard of his laptop. 'Anything you can give us on Colonel Holliday' s whereabouts, Roger?'

'Just this,' said the analyst. He hit a key and a video image appeared on the wall-sized screen at the far end of the room. 'We piggyback the American weather satellites as a matter of course. We intercepted this about ten minutes ago. It's thermal; everything else was obscured by the heavy rainfall.'

The screen showed a psychedelic multicolored view from about a hundred feet overhead as a large, twin-engine aircraft headed in for a landing. Almost directly in front of it was the outline of a large automobile, the engine glowing bright red and almost obscuring the two blobs of heat within it.

The shape of the airplane suddenly began to pirouette, one of the wings and its engine colliding directly with the automobile, the explosion of the engine obscuring the shape of the vehicle, which suddenly blossomed into a spreading heat pattern.

The aircraft eventually stopped and after a moment four heat traces began to move away from it at a run.

A hundred yards away from the downed plane, the four heat traces stopped and then disappeared within a slightly larger one that began to move away from the scene. The image went blank.

'What exactly did we just see?' Sir Alistair asked.

Thornhill explained, 'An aircraft, probably an old DC3, belly-landed at a small airfield near Bayou La Batre, Alabama – Bayou La Batre is where they shot the shrimp boat scenes in *Forrest Gump*, by the way. At any rate, as it landed one wing of the downed aircraft swung around and slammed into a waiting vehicle, either a Cadillac Escalade or a limousine, from the size of the heat signature.

'In the process the two passengers inside the vehicle were killed by the resulting explosion. The plane comes to rest and a few moments later four people exit the DC3 and run to a waiting panel van, something the size of a Renault Kangoo or a Ford Transit. Once in the van, they start it up and drive off.'

'And what on earth does this have to do with our Colonel Holliday?' Givens, the man from the Home Office, asked.

'Do shut up, won't you?' Sir Alistair said. He turned to Thornhill. 'Go on, then, Roger.'

'This might explain things a little better,' said the analyst. He tapped a few keys on his computer, and a still image appeared on the big screen. 'We know Holliday and his people have crossed swords with

Kate Sinclair in all her incarnations, and we also know that Holliday has been seen in northern Brazil – Amazonia to be precise, an area with direct ties to our own Lord Grayle and the Pallas Group. This shot was taken fifteen minutes before the tropical storm now known as Mellissa struck Bayou La Batre.' The image now on the screen showed a limousine with a well-dressed man standing beside it smoking a cigarette or a cigar.

'Can we come in a little closer on that?' Sir Alistair said.

Roger Thornhill tapped another key.

The photograph zoomed in.

'Oh dear,' Sir Alistair sighed. 'Charles Peace.'

26

It took them slightly more than twelve hours to make the trip to Miami, stopping only six times, three at public rest stops and twice for food at a Denny's and once at a Harvey's BBQ for a rib-tip sandwich.

The address they were looking for was farther down Old Cutler Road in Coral Gables and through the fairy-tale arch of giant banyan trees that turned the street into a dappled tunnel, brightening as the sun rose.

It was seven thirty in the morning when they found the address Rafi was looking for. It was an old rancher from the Sixties fronted by a forest of untended trees and foliage, the house barely visible from the street.

They turned down the driveway and climbed out of the van into the misty air. They walked up to the front door and Rafi knocked. A few moments later there was the sound of feet shuffling in slippers. The door opened.

'A change of name or place may sometimes save a person,' Rafi said, then repeated the phrase in Hebrew.

'*Eyn ashan bli esh,*' said the man.

'There is no smoke without fire.'

The man sighed and ushered them into the house. 'Feh,' the man said. 'Just what I need, guests at this hour of the day, countersigns so old they have dust on them. You'll be hungry. I'll give you breakfast.'

He turned away, then led them across an old man's living room of comfortable furniture, walls of books and framed photographs and newspapers strewn across a floor covered by an old braided rug.

'My name is Avrom Lazar, by the way. I teach Judaic studies at the University of Miami. I am only a spy in my spare time. A *sayani*, as we are called.'

The kitchen could have been teleported from the Fifties, complete with pale yellow cupboards and appliances, cottage curtains with cornflower blue patterns and a yellow Formica table, six matching vinyl chairs and a checkerboard black-and-white linoleum floor.

Avrom Lazar busied himself around the kitchen making breakfast, humming quietly. Even at this early hour, he was wearing a yarmulke pinned to unruly silver hair. He was in his eighties with drooping bags beneath twinkling eyes and rosy cheeks forced down by time and gravity on either side of an almost feminine mouth that looked as though it rarely frowned.

The man had bright red reading glasses perched on his forehead and wore a brown corduroy suit much too warm for the summer, complete with vest, white shirt and tie, the vest decorated with a fob and chain that spanned a moderate belly. He wore purple velvet bedroom slippers.

Breakfast turned out to be toasted bagels with deli cream cheese, a lox and green onion omelet and an endless supply of excellent coffee. They told their story as they ate. Lazar said nothing, merely nodding from time to time.

Using a laptop she'd purchased at a Walmart Supercenter in Panama City, Peggy showed him the photographs she'd transferred from her camera on to a memory stick revealing the inside of Hiram's ossuary, and he just nodded again.

When they'd finished their story, Lazar took an old briar pipe from the pocket of his jacket, put in a large pinch of some aromatic blend he kept in a leather pouch and lit up with a kitchen match he fired on a thick yellowed thumbnail.

'What a wonderful tale,' he said, puffing on the pipe. 'Rather reminiscent of Steven Spielberg at his best. I would have loved to be with you on such an adventure. I haven't done something as exciting as that since the war.'

'You fought in World War Two?' Holliday asked.

'Fought is hardly the word. I was initially part of the Jewish Brigade Group and then I was sent over to British Intelligence because of my knowledge of European art.'

'Art?' Peggy said.

'I was studying at the Slade when the war broke out. My intention was to write the definitive biography of Constable since I had no artistic talent myself, but SIS was already interested in Adolf's looting even early in the war and they recruited me. Following the end of the conflict, I was the handler for several field groups, one of whom had the mandate of discovering the source, if any, of Hitler's acquisition of religious relics – the Ark of the Covenant in particular.'

'Uncle Henry,' said Holliday.

'Quite so,' said Lazar. 'Henry Granger and Derek Carr-Harris.' He turned to Rafi. 'Do you know what your father did just after the war, Dr Wanounou?'

'He was an archaeologist. He died when I was sixteen.'

'Were you aware that his first dig was at Khirbet Qumran in 1947 under the direction of a Dominican priest named Roland de Vaux?'

'Is this going where I think it's going?' Holliday asked.

'I don't get it,' said Peggy.

'There was a man, a Cistercian monk named Bernard de Clairvaux, who wrote the Templar creed. He was really the first Templar. You're trying to say there's a connection between the two men?' Holliday explained.

'A direct descendant. Roland de Vaux spent his first years at the *École biblique et archéologique française de Jérusalem* studying the old documents relating to the Templars,' said Lazar.

'It sparked his interest in two things – the ruins on top of the cliffs at Qumran and an obscure Templar knight named Sir William Fitzmartin. Fitzmartin was a monk of the Abbey of St Andrew. All we know of him is that he vanished sometime shortly after the taking of Jerusalem in 1099. He is notable for refusing to take part in the massacre that followed the siege and was last seen to be headed into the Eastern Desert, alone. According to Roland de Vaux, his family sigil, a single lion rampant below a Templar cross, was found scratched on to a staircase in the ruins of the Scriptorium at Khirbet Qumran.'

'What does any of this have to do with my father?' Rafi asked.

'He was the one who found Fitzmartin's mark.'

'So when you cut to the chase, you're saying you believe the Ark exists,' Holliday said.

'Of course it exists,' replied Lazar. 'We've known about it for years. That's one of the major reasons we've been excavating around the Dome of the Rock for the past ten years. If you asked the average American who should own the Ark, he'd tell you it's a Christian relic when of course it's not. Moses led the Jews out of Egypt, not the Christians. Christ was a

Jew, after all. The Ark belongs in Israel, not to the Vatican, and certainly not to Kate Sinclair. It's ours. We'd like you to get it back.'

'You knew we'd come here?' Rafi asked.

'I was advised that it was a probability.'

'Mossad has been watching us?'

'Since the monk Rodrigues gave you the notebook on the island of Corvo.'

'So what do we do now?' Holliday said.

'First we must get you out of the United States and into Israel. We can't fly you out of any of the major airports. Security is too tough. I suggest Canada.'

'We'll need documents.'

'Easy enough. You'll each cross separately from Detroit to Windsor by car. I have access to a private jet from one of our other "friends" here in Miami. It's all been arranged. I just have to say the word.'

'Then say it.' Holliday nodded.

'I have never been to Israel,' said Eddie.

'You'll love it,' said Holliday. 'Just like Cuba – hot weather and white sand beaches.'

Antonio Ruffino sat in Lord Adrian Grayle's library, a snifter of very expensive Rémy Martin in one hand and a Cuban Bolívar in the other. He was staring at the immense three-by-five painting of a battle. It was incredibly detailed, horses rearing, men dying, cannons blasting.

'William Sadler, *The Battle of Waterloo*,' said Grayle, spritzing a little soda into his glass of Scotch. 'We won, if you'll recall.'

'I have never been in your home without the others. I am wondering why I have been singled out for brandy and cigars. It is a great honor, Lord Grayle.'

Grayle was perfectly aware of the slightly acidic tone in the Italian's voice. 'I want you to deliver a message to your brother, the cardinal secretary of state,' Grayle said bluntly.

'You know I am not on good terms with my brother, for obvious reasons.'

'Your brother has assets available to him that I do not and vice versa. We must use those assets to defeat a common enemy.'

'What enemy?'

'Holliday and his people. Everyone is after them now. They're on their way to Israel as we speak. They're too close. We have to stop them from reaching their objective. Stop them dead.'

27

The plateau of Khirbet Qumran lies less than fifteen miles from the high hills of Jerusalem and less than two miles from the shores of the Dead Sea. The entire area is a national park, complete with an interpretive visitors' center and an oversized tour bus parking lot.

There were no tour buses today and very few tourists. The sun was a white-hot furnace in a sky leached of any color. It was over a hundred and ten in the shade of the few palms that grew on the fringes of the parking lot, and a steady wind from the south was blowing up clouds of dust. Holliday and the others had come prepared, and as they climbed out of the rental van they were wearing kaffiyehs and Ryder sand goggles they'd purchased at a Jerusalem motorcycle store.

'I feel like one of the sand people in *Star Wars*,' said Peggy.

'You look like a teeny, tiny Anwar Sadat,' joked Rafi.

'I'm still not talking to you, Mr Mossad agent,' Peggy snorted back. She was hauling a small plastic cooler out of the back of the van. It was stuffed with water bottles and protein bars for all of them. There were even a few oranges.

Rafi sighed. 'I'm not a Mossad agent, Peg. I'm a *sayan*, just like Avrom Lazar. A helper when I'm needed, no more than that.'

'Whatever,' said Peggy. 'The point is, you should have told me.'

'They told me not to.'

'They?'

'Mossad,' he answered, sighing again.

'Then you really are a Mossad agent.'

Holliday broke in. 'This is going nowhere. Enough domestic disputes. Which way are the ruins?'

'This way,' said Rafi. 'I'll lead the way.' He picked up the gym bag carrying his basic 'dig' tools and they headed toward the ruins.

Khirbet Qumran was occupied during the first century BC as a place of refuge by the Essenes, a group of Jewish holy men who decided that Jerusalem and the Temple had become a place of sin and corruption, much as Christ did a hundred and thirty years later. The occupants of the community, all men, numbered a thousand at the high point of the settlement, and these men spent much of their time transcribing the early Scriptures on to parchment and keeping the settlement self-sustaining by the use of an aqueduct to capture water from the regular flash floods that struck the area as well as raising sheep for both sustenance and for the parchment made from the animal skins. They were also well-known potters and provided water jars for the other communities along the coast.

With the arrival of the Romans in 68 BC, things became much more tenuous for the Essene community, and to prevent the destruction of the Scriptures and other documents relating to their creed, they began a steady program of putting these documents in sealed pottery jars and hiding them in the caves of the surrounding hills. The Essenes faded into history, but miraculously the documents remained hidden until they were accidentally discovered in 1946 by Muhammad Ahmed al-Hamed, better known by his nickname Muhammed edh-Dhib ('Muhammad the Wolf'), a Bedouin shepherd boy from the Ta'amireh clan residing in Bethlehem. These were the famous Dead Sea Scrolls, which in many ways rewrote what was known about the Old Testament as well as the history of Judaism at the time they were written.

They reached the ruins, an unprepossessing scattering of piled rocks and stones, whatever mortar had held them together as walls long eaten away by the sand, wind and the passage of time. An unlikely place to find the most valuable relic in both the Christian and Hebrew worlds.

The group stood there, muffled against the grating of the blowing sand, staring at the ruins through the eerily tinted lenses of their goggles.

'Beautiful,' said Rafi. Holliday knew he wasn't seeing ruins but the buildings as they had been all those centuries ago. He saw it peopled with men as they went about the business of the settlement, heard the sound of potters' wheels and the chants of holy men at prayer. Holliday had felt something like it in his time: the stamping of Nazi jackboots on the Champs-Élysées, the clatter of arrows raining down from a castle parapet in Spain, the thunder of horses crossing the blood-soaked fields of Waterloo. Sometimes the power of history could reach out from the distant past and touch you, if only for a moment. To Rafi this moment was magical.

'Where did they find this sign of the knight?' Eddie asked.

Rafi pointed through the swirling cloud of sand to the rear of the settlement. 'There,' he said, his voice muffled by the kaffiyeh. 'The smallest of the cisterns, close to the aqueduct. At the foot of the staircase leading down to the water.'

They plodded through the ruins, skirting walls, cutting through the remains of roofless, doorless buildings.

'This is what we call in Spanish *fantasmal*.'

'Spooky,' said Holliday.

'*Sí, mi coronel, muy* spooky. Bad spirits are here. There were hard deaths in this place.'

'He's right,' said Rafi as they made their way through the ruins. 'In the first century AD the Romans destroyed this place and slaughtered every Jew they could find. Same old, same old.'

They finally reached their destination at the far end of the settlement. It was a series of three small cisterns, the main one in the middle being fed by the aqueduct overhead, the main pool feeding the two others, one left and one right.

The pools were clearly man-made, roughly circular pits about eight feet deep and lined with bricks. A stairway led down to the bottom of the pool, and two more stairways, no more than three or four steps, led down to the deeper pools on either side.

'The knight's scratches are at the foot of the stairs leading to the left pool,' said Rafi, pointing.

They climbed slowly down the crumbling steps, then went down the four steps leading to the smaller pool. It was roughly circular, carved out of the sandstone and lined with bricks. Rafi knelt down at the base of the short flight of steps, opened his gym bag and took out a broad hard-bristle paintbrush. He gently teased the buildup of sand away from the bottom step until a faint image appeared.

'Hand me a bottle of water please,' he said to Peggy. She opened the cooler and cracked open a small bottle of Mey Eden mineral water. He sprinkled it over the deeply etched stone, and the image became clear – a childlike figure of a lion with a larger and very distinct Templar Cross above it.

Rafi sat back on his haunches as the others stooped to see the marking. Below the level of the plateau, the sand blew more softly and the wind was less, so Rafi pulled his goggles down to see better. The others followed suit.

'There have always been different interpretations other than the fact that a Knight Templar was here. Was it Sir William Fitzmartin himself, or simply one of the other knights he recruited to come with him on the Crusade? Was it no more than a piece of errant and idle graffiti by a man in Fitzmartin's band who simply paused here for a cup of water? The arguments have been going back and forth since De Vaux found the sign on his early excavations here. There are even some of his enemies who whispered that he had scratched the marks there himself to bolster his reputation.'

'Could it have been?'

'According to his journals of the dig, my father thought so. Initially De Vaux had given him the job of digging at the pool site, which was hardly the jewel of the operation. De Vaux was a vain and egotistical man, but he was also a shrewd man. To have found the sigil himself would have been suspicious; having a young student like my father find it made the discovery much more feasible as the real thing.'

'Your father was a suspicious man,' said Eddie, smiling.

'A suspicious mind in an archaeologist is a good thing.'

'And in a Mossad agent,' grumbled Peggy.

'I have not been, am not now and will never be a Mossad agent,' said Rafi.

'Can it,' said Holliday. 'We have to stay focused. Why this place? Is there anything special about it?'

'There are arguments about that, as well.'

'What arguments?'

'Why three pools, why so close to the aqueduct – it runs right above us – and why are they so small in relation to the half dozen other cisterns scattered throughout the community?'

'You have a theory?'

'Yes, but it's not readily accepted.'

'Why?'

'I think it's a *mikvah*, a ritual cleansing pool. The three pools together, their lack of depth in relation to the other cisterns and the fact that these were very holy men. The *mikvah* would be a necessary ritual every day, and this is the most likely spot.'

The wind began picking up again, roaring over the plateau and driving what few tourists had come for a visit back to their cars. Holliday felt the hairs on the back of his neck rising, and all his senses were suddenly on high alert. He felt terribly exposed. Maybe it was just Eddie's *fantasmal*, and maybe not.

He felt the Cuban's big black hand grip his shoulder. 'I feel it, too, amigo,' he said quietly.

Holliday dragged himself back to the matter at hand. 'What are the arguments against its being a *mikvah*?'

'Theoretically a *mikvah* must have running water; a man cannot cleanse himself in the taint of the previous user. None of the three pools has running water available; like all the other cisterns, they are merely vessels for storing water.'

'What would it take to make this running water?' Holliday asked.

Eddie shrugged. 'Every bathtub must have a plug, yes?'

'A drain,' said Peggy.

'There is no drain,' Rafi said.

'To prove your theory is correct, there has to be a drain, right?'

'But there isn't one. They've gone over this settlement a thousand times in the past eighty years. They would have found a drain if there was one.'

'Just like they didn't find the Dead Sea Scrolls for two millennia,' said Holliday.

'So, what's the answer?' Peggy asked.

'I know what he is going to say,' said Eddie, rolling his eyes and grinning.

'So what am I going to say, you Cuban *sabelotodo*?' asked Holliday.

'Your Cuban is getting real good, *mi coronel*.'

'Answer the question, smart-ass.'

'When you have eliminated the impossible, whatever remains, however improbable, must be the truth,' quoted Eddie. 'Your favorite saying of the great detective Mr Sherlock Holmes.'

'Okay, then, where is the drain?' Rafi demanded, sweeping his arm around the twelve-foot-diameter pool.

Holliday thought for a moment, letting his mind wander over the whole problem and its possible answer. He had a glimmering of something, but he couldn't quite see it. 'It can't be a drain,' he said finally.

'Really helpful,' said Rafi.

'Think about it. How were these baths used? What did the people do?'

'They stripped off their clothes, then immersed themselves.'

'How much of themselves?'

'Total immersion was the prescribed way if it was possible, like the original baptisms. Total immersion and then a rebirth without your sins.'

'So they'd come down the steps until they were completely underwater.'

'Presumably.' Rafi nodded.

'But how?'

'I don't understand.'

'They must have had a way of filling the pool, using the aqueduct, or drawing it from the other cisterns, right?' Holliday paused. 'They had to fill it up, probably almost up to the top step.' He indicated the top of the pool a few feet above their heads.

'Obviously,' said Rafi. 'We've been over this.'

'Would they use the same water over and over again to bathe themselves?'

'That makes no sense,' said Eddie.

'So that means they had to empty it,' said Holliday.

'Through a nonexistent drain,' said Rafi.

'Which would be like emptying a bathtub; it hardly rates as running water,' Holliday said.

'So?' Peggy asked.

'Richard Nixon,' said Holliday.

'*Qué?*' Eddie said.

'A water gate. The Egyptians had them for irrigation. Like the floodgates on a dam. They'd have a series of pulleys to raise and lower it; as the holy men came into the water, the gate would be slowly opened, letting the water rush out in a controlled way. Running water.'

'I don't see anything,' Peggy said, staring.

'I do,' said Rafi. He had his paintbrush and water bottle out and began brushing dust and old mortar away from the side of the stairwell. It didn't take very much time at all. Within fifteen minutes he'd dis-

262

covered a section on the side of the stairway seven feet high and three feet wide.

'Bricks, not stones,' he said. 'Put in a long time after the pool was built. He stared at what he had discovered, shaking his head. 'It was probably sealed up by Fitzmartin or whoever left that sign. A thousand years and nobody noticed.'

'Nobody was looking for it,' said Holliday.

Rafi stood back and examined the section of brick wall revealed by his water and his paintbrush. 'This hardly rates as accepted archaeological practice, but what the hell?' He raised his leg and slammed at the brickwork with the sole of his heavy hiking boot. The brickwork, its mortar decayed or nonexistent, crumbled under the attack. A hole appeared with nothing but darkness behind. The others joined in and soon the opening was big enough to step through. Rafi fished a large Maglite out of his bag and switched it on.

'Come on,' he said, 'let's see what's on the other side.'

28

Stepping through the ragged hole in the brickwork, they suddenly found themselves in a cool, slightly damp environment filled with the faintly comforting scent of a basement that was something just short of paradise after the savage heat and the blowing sandstorm they'd left behind them.

As they walked through the darkness, guided by the cold circle of light produced by Rafi's flashlight, a few details came to light. The tunnel or watercourse or whatever it was had a hewn stone floor and was built as a single arch with quarried stone of some kind other than the local material of the plateau. The stones were fitted together perfectly without a crack between them, perhaps a faint reminder of an earlier period of history when Hebrew hands had built the pyramids of Egypt. Was this the work of the descendants of Moses' people, led out of the Pharaoh's land and into the desert?

'Real masons,' said Peggy. 'This wasn't done by men in funny hats and barbecue aprons.'

'Put this on the History Channel and they'd build a whole story around alien plumbers. Fit you in right between *American Pickers* and *Cajun Pawn Stars*,' grunted Holliday.

The passage branched several times, but inevitably the roving circle of light would find the Templar cross and the lion rampant guiding the way.

'He's leaving us a trail of breadcrumbs,' said Rafi. 'The question is, where is he leading us?'

'Maybe he's leading us to Harrison Ford.'

'Peggy?' Holliday said.

'Yes?'

'Shut up.'

'You know how I get when I'm in little dark spaces.'

'Shut up anyway.'

'Okay, Doc.'

The passage seemed to both narrow and become less high. Both Eddie and Holliday were forced to stoop, and all of them could feel their shoulders brushing the side walls.

'I don't like this,' said Peggy, her voice beginning to quaver. The jokes were gone.

'Relax,' said Rafi. 'It's just the Bernoulli effect. They turned this part of the aqueduct into a venturi tube.'

'Liquids forced through a narrower channel increase in speed,' said Holliday.

'I knew that,' said Peggy

'They knew about this so long ago?' Eddie asked.

'They didn't know the theory. It was all observation. I'll bet you we're going up an incline. To give the water the velocity necessary to overcome gravity, they narrowed the conduit.'

A hundred feet farther on, the tunnel opened up and they could walk freely. Holliday could actually feel a slight incline, and then the tunnel branched again. Fitzmartin's sign was there to guide them again, so they turned to the right. Another hundred feet and they were suddenly faced with an obstacle that appeared impossible to overcome.

'The ceiling collapsed,' said Rafi, pointing the Maglite at an enormous pile of rock and stone barring their way.

'The collapse could be yards thick; there's no way we can clear it,' Holliday said.

'Any sign of the knight's mark?' Peggy asked.

Rafi swung the flashlight beam around.

'There!' Eddie said, pointing. On the right side of the collapse, barely visible, was the top half of the Templar cross. Eddie scrambled up the pile of fallen rock. He began to hand the fallen stones down to Rafi and Holliday, who piled them off to one side. Eventually the Cuban had revealed the top of a narrow arch.

'Give me the flashlight please,' said Eddie. Rafi handed it up and Eddie poked the beam into the opening.

'What can you see?' Holliday called up the pile.

'A ladder,' he said. 'A ladder of iron rungs set into the stone. Very old and very rusty.'

'How high?'

'Twenty meters, maybe a little more,' said Eddie. 'The light does not reach the top.'

'What's that in American?' Peggy asked.

'Sixty-five feet, give or take a few inches,' answered Rafi.

'No way, José. This place is bad enough. You won't get Maggie Blackstock's baby girl climbing any two-thousand-year-old rusty ladder.'

'Harrison Ford would do it,' teased Holliday. 'He does all his own stunts.'

'Yeah, and he's getting thirty million a pop for each movie he's in. No chance I'm going up that ladder.'

Eddie had already enlarged the aperture. Within five minutes there was a hole they could squeeze through.

'Coming?' Holliday asked as Rafi scrambled up the tumble of stone and vanished into the hole.

'Oh, crap,' said Peggy. 'Of course I am.'

She followed Holliday up the rocks and slipped in through the hole.

The chimney up through the stone of the Khirbet Qumran plateau was a rough oval eight feet across, and natural rather than hewn by man's hand. On the right a strange climbing apparatus had been bolted to the stone. A ladder had been created by attaching a series of long lengths of iron together, bolting those lengths into the rock, then driving iron bars through the lengths at right angles to form a long procession of T rungs that disappeared up into the darkness.

'It's a "compline ladder,"' said Rafi, shining his light on the ancient ironwork. The hammer marks of the long-dead blacksmith were still visible.

'A what?'

'The old Hermetics used them to climb down into their holes or up into their caves. They were usually made of wood because that's all they had at hand. Some sects even think it is a symbolic image of the Crucifixion. In monastic terms it represents Jacob's ladder, the story told within the call to evening prayer.'

'So, who goes first?' Peggy asked.

'You do,' said Rafi.

'You're kidding.'

'You're the lightest, then me, then Doc and then Eddie. Relax, kiddo. We'll be right behind you. I won't let you fall.'

'Just don't look down, right?'

'I wouldn't recommend it.'

They began to climb, Peggy's breathing becoming more ragged with each rung. Behind her Rafi's wobbling light guided the way upward. Several times Peggy froze, the creaking of the bolts holding the rusted contrivance to the rock wall grinding and half pulling out of their settings in the stone. Rafi calmly urged her on and one by one they reached the summit.

Rafi switched off the light as he came up through the narrow orifice. 'It's a cave,' he said, calling down to Holliday and Eddie. It was small, barely high enough for Holliday and Eddie to stand upright, the walls and ceiling covered with some sort of gray-brown stuccolike substance that had cracked and broken off with time. Enough light came in through the cave entrance to light the full interior. From the sight lines of the opening, which extended to the steep side of the plateau as well as the hills far beyond, Holliday could see that the entrance would be almost always in shadow, invisible except for brief moments during the day. The wind howled around the entrance like a living thing, fighting to get inside.

'It's empty,' Peggy said, looking around. 'We went through all that to find an empty cave? Was this Fitz-martin guy playing a joke, or what?'

'I don't think so,' said Rafi. 'Look at the wall.'

'I see it,' said Holliday.

Rafi slipped the pack off his back and dug around, coming up with a small rock hammer. Here and there deep scratches on the stone were revealed by the flaking off of the stucco.

Rafi went to work, using the hammer to gently break away the fragile stucco, revealing several lines of strange-looking characters that had been etched into the wall of the cave two thousand years before.

'What is it?' Holliday asked.

'Nabatean Aramaic,' said Rafi.

'The language used by the people of Jerusalem and the Essenes at the time of Christ,' said Holliday.

'Can you read it?' asked Holliday.

'It's not the whole message. There's more beneath it.'

Rafi spent another few minutes chipping off the last of the stucco, revealing the entire message. The final blow of the hammer was enough to break off a large section of the stucco, exposing some kind of niche cut into the wall below it.

'Chicken tracks,' said Peggy, staring at the squiggly series of lines on the wall.

'What does it say?' Holliday asked.

Rafi studied the message again, his lips moving slightly as he formed and translated the ancient message.

'It says, "The King of the Jews is dead. The Messiah is reborn in the East."'

'There is a box in the opening beneath the message,' said Eddie, pointing.

Between them the three men managed to pull the stone box out of the niche and place it carefully on the floor. The box was a little more than two feet long and about eighteen inches high. The top was a loosely fitted slab of the same kind of stone. Inside was a collection of old bones without a skull and a few scraps of fabric or what might have been skin or parchment.

'It's an ossuary,' said Rafi. 'Bodies would be entombed until decomposition was complete and a year or so later the bones would be placed in a box like this and taken to a crypt of some kind.'

'Any idea who the bones belong to?'

'Given the message on the wall, I can hazard a guess,' Rafi said. He went back to his pack and brought out his bristle paintbrush. He turned the ossuary on its side and gently eased away the dust of centuries. A simple line of lettering appeared, this time in what Holliday thought looked like some form of ancient Hebrew.

yeshua ben yosef

'Yeshua Ben Yosef, Joshua, son of Joseph, Christ's name before the world and the Greek translators got to it,' Rafi said. 'The relic, the Ark of the Covenant, vanished with Christ into the East, and somehow Fitzmartin knew where.'

Suddenly the wind dropped and the cave was flooded with light. Peggy went to the mouth of the cave and stared out, shading her eyes. 'Would you look at that?' she said, smiling and turning back to look at Rafi and the others. 'All of a sudden it's a beautiful day out there.'

Without a sound the large-caliber sniper's bullet struck at the base of Peggy's cervical spine before exploding out through her neck in a haze of blood. She never heard the sound of the echoing shot that killed her so quickly it was as though her soul leaped out of her body so fiercely she simply dropped in place, the smile still on her ruined face.

'Peggy!' Rafi screamed, standing and hurling himself toward her curled-up figure on the floor of the cave.

'Rafi! No!' Holliday yelled.

Rafi reached Peggy's body, a wailing scream rising from deep within him. He leaned forward, pressing his hand over the ragged hole in her throat, trying to stop blood that had already ceased to flow. Holliday crawled toward them on his elbows and knees. 'Get down!'

The second shot was a little off center, catching Rafi under his left lung, splintering ribs and tearing down through his kidney and spleen, the rest of his vital organs struck by sharp shards of his splintered ribs. He gave a single heaving breath of surprise, slumping down beside Peggy, what was left of his lungs heaving, forcing blood up his gullet and into his mouth.

The sound of the shot echoed, and then there was a screaming cluster of shots that struck the interior of the small space like a swarm of angry hornets. Then there was silence.

Holliday's brain worked without conscious thought. *Twelve hundred yards, he's firing at shadows. A pro special forces from some army. Super sniper; a few of those in Vietnam, more now after Iraq and Afghanistan. He won't hang around.* Still, Holliday kept low, finally reaching Rafi and Peggy. Rafi was still breathing, but barely. There was no hope for him; he was going to die and he knew it. He reached up and grabbed Holliday's hand.

'Don't . . . don't let them get away with this. Don't let them find the Ark. Nobody should have that kind of power.' He coughed out a gout of blood that painted his chest glistening red. 'Promise me.'

'I promise,' said Holliday, gripping Rafi's hand. He watched the light fade in the archaeologist's eyes, but he held his hand for a few moments longer, making sure Rafi felt a friend's touch as he died. He turned then and, weeping, stared down at Peggy. He reached out and softly touched her hair. 'I promise,' he said.

Holliday felt Eddie's gentle hand on his shoulder.

'I am so sorry, my friend.'

'So am I,' said Holliday, roughly wiping away his tears.

'So what now, *mi coronel?*'

Holliday's eyes were hard. 'I keep my promise. We find the Ark and then we kill them all.'

PAUL CHRISTOPHER

THE TEMPLAR CROSS

Some secrets are too great to bear

Army Ranger Lt. Col. John 'Doc' Holliday is teaching at West Point when he receives desperate news. His niece Peggy has been kidnapped while joining an ancient tomb excavation in Egypt.

Holliday immediately sets out to locate and rescue her. But Peggy's captors belong to the Brotherhood of the Temple of Isis - murderous fanatics who worship a dead god.

A trail of clues sends Holliday deep into Africa and into the heart of a conspiracy involving an ancient Egyptian legend and the darkest secrets of the Order of Templar Knights.

Secrets that, once uncovered, are a death warrant . . .

PAUL CHRISTOPHER

THE TEMPLAR THRONE

The hidden hand which rules history . . .

Army Ranger John Holliday has made it his life's mission to unlock the secrets of the ruthless, ancient Templar Order, who are as renowned for their hidden wealth and power as for their desperate secrecy.

In *The Templar Throne* his quest has him crisscrossing Europe and the US hunting for the True Ark – a box reputed to hold precious holy relics and the Templars' most powerful secrets. But Holliday's hunt is also a deadly chase. On the trail of the relics are the Vatican Secret Service, the CIA and an arcane brotherhood of Templar descendants who know just how much power the Ark holds.

And they'll kill anyone in their way . . .

PAUL CHRISTOPHER

THE TEMPLAR CONSPIRACY

The ruthless reign of a secret power must be stopped . . .

In Rome, the public assassination of the Pope by a sniper on Christmas Day sets off a massive investigation that stretches across the globe. But behind the veil of Rex Deus – the Templar cabal that silently wields power in the twenty-first century – the plot has only just begun.

The cabal has a position of ultimate control in its sights – and its head, Kate Sinclair, is never going to yield her one great ambition for her US senator son, Richard Pierce Sinclair.

When ex-Army Ranger John Holliday uncovers the true motive behind the Pontiff's murder, he must unlock the secrets of a modern Templar conspiracy – and unravel Kate Sinclair's deadly design.

PAUL CHRISTOPHER

THE TEMPLAR LEGION

The hunter becomes the hunted.

Army Ranger Lt. Col. John Holliday continues his quest to uncover the mysterious secrets of the ancient Templar Order, an organization renowned for its incredible wealth and hidden power.

Holliday is swept into an adventure as deadly as it is secretive when an archaeologist friend makes a bizarre find in Ethiopia. But when he follows a trail of clues through the chaotic and lawless horn of Africa, Holliday finds himself hunted by a ruthless foe, as he comes closer and closer to a priceless treasure . . . an ancient artefact that can only be found by those who can solve a riddle from the past.

But his pursuers will stop at nothing to get it first . . .

PAUL CHRISTOPHER

RED TEMPLAR

Army Ranger and historian John Holliday has spent his life crossing the globe uncovering the truth behind the ancient Templar Order. Now, finally returning home, he is intercepted by a mysterious Russian, Genrikhovich, with an astonishing secret.

Genrikhovick claims to know the location of the long-lost Templar sword, Aos – one of four taken from the Holy Land and the fall of Acre. He believes it is the companion of Holliday's own Templar sword. Holliday is sent out on a deadly and bloody quest in the dark heart of Russia, where the Templars have wielded power for centuries.

But can Genrikhovich be trusted? Will Holliday's search for the truth finally kill him? And what is the greatest Templar secret of all?

PAUL CHRISTOPHER

VALLEY OF THE TEMPLARS

Retired Army Ranger John Holliday and his friend Eddie travel to Cuba in search of Eddie's mysteriously vanished brother-and find themselves desperately trying to stop a shocking plot of a secret Templar cabal that has been growing for five hundred years.

As the conspiracy tightens the corrupt and dying Castro regime in an iron grip, Holliday must find Eddie's brother before it is too late . . . and the secret horror of what lies in the Valley of Death is revealed.